I0684636

Fanny, the Flower-Girl

Selina Bunbury

Contents

FANNY, THE FLOWER-GIRL

BY

Selina Bunbury

FANNY, THE FLOWER-GIRL

C ome, buy my flowers; flowers fresh and fair. Come, buy my flowers. Please ma'am, buy a nice bunch of flowers, very pretty ones, ma'am. Please, sir, to have some flowers; nice, fresh ones, miss; only just gathered; please look."

Thus spoke, or sometimes sung, a little girl of perhaps eight years old, holding in her hand a neat small basket, on the top of which lay a clean white cloth, to shade from the sun the flowers which she praised so highly, and a little bunch of which she presented to almost every passer-by, in the hope of finding purchasers; while, after one had passed rudely on, another had looked at her young face and smiled, another had said, "What a nice child!" but not one had taken the flowers, and left the penny or the half-penny that was to pay for them the little girl, as if accustomed to all this, only arranged again the pretty nosegays that had been disarranged in the vain hope of selling them, and commenced anew in her pretty singing tone, "Come, buy my flowers; flowers fresh and fair."

"Your flowers are sadly withered, my little maid," said a kind, country-looking gentleman, who was buying some vegetables at a stall near her.

"Oh, sir! I have fresh ones, here, sir; please look;" and the child lifted up the cover of her basket, and drew from the very bottom a bunch of blossoms on which the dew of morning still rested.

"Please to see, sir; a pretty rose, sir, and these pinks and mignonette, and a bunch of jessamine, sir, and all for one penny."

"Bless thee! pretty dear!" said the old lame vegetable-seller, "thou'lt make a good market-woman one of these days. Your honor would do well to buy her flowers, sir, she has got no mother or father, God help her, and works for a sick grandmother."

"Poor child!" said the old gentleman. "Here, then, little one, give me three nice nosegays, and there is sixpence for you."

With delight sparkling in every feature of her face, and her color changed to crimson with joy, the little flower-girl received in one hand the unusual piece of money; and setting her basket on the ground, began hastily and tremblingly to pick out nearly half its contents as the price of the sixpence; but the gentleman stooped down, and taking up at random three bunches of the flowers, which were not the freshest, said,

"Here, these will do; keep the rest for a more difficult customer. Be a good child; pray to God, and serve Him, and you will find He is the Father of the fatherless."

And so he went away; and the flower-girl, without waiting to put her basket in order, turned to the old vegetable-seller, and cried, "Sixpence! a whole sixpence, and all at once. What will grandmother say now? See!" and opening her hand, she displayed its shining before her neighbor's eyes.

"Eh!" exclaimed the old man, as he approached his eyes nearer to it. "Eh! what is this? why thou hast twenty sixpences there; this is a half-sovereign!"

"Twenty sixpences! why the gentleman said, there is sixpence for thee," said the child.

"Because he didn't know his mistake," replied the other; "I saw him take the piece out of his waistcoat-pocket without looking."

"Oh dear! what shall I do?" cried the little girl.

"Why, thou must keep it, to be sure," replied the old man; "give it to thy grandmother, she will know what to do with it, I warrant thee."

"But I must first try to find the good gentleman, and tell him of his mistake," said the child. "I know what grandmother would say else; and he cannot be far off, I think, because he was so fat; he will go slow, I am sure, this hot morning. Here, Mr. Williams, take care of my basket, please, till I come back."

And without a word more, the flower-girl put down her little basket at the foot of the vegetable-stall, and ran away as fast as she could go.

When she turned out of the market-place, she found, early as it was, that the street before her was pretty full; but as from the passage the gentleman had taken to leave the market-place, she knew he could only have gone in one direction, she had still hopes of finding him; and she ran on and on, until she actually thought she saw the very person before her; he had just taken off his hat, and was wiping his forehead with his handkerchief.

"That is him," said the little flower-girl, "I am certain;" but just as she spoke, some persons came between her and the gentleman, and she could not see him. Still she kept running on; now passing off the foot-path into the street, and then seeing the fat gentleman still before her; and then again getting on the foot-path, and losing sight of him, until at last she came up quite close to him, as he was walking slowly, and wiping the drops of heat from his forehead.

The poor child was then quite out of breath; and when she got up to him she could not call out to him to stop, nor say one word; so she caught hold of the skirt of his coat, and gave it a strong pull.

The gentleman started, and clapped one hand on his coat-pocket, and raised up his cane in the other, for he was quite sure it was a pickpocket at his coat. But when he turned, he saw the breathless little flower-girl, and he looked rather sternly at her, and said,

"Well, what do you want; what are you about? eh!"

"Oh, sir!" said the girl; and then she began to cough, for her breath was quite spent. "See, sir; you said you gave me sixpence, and Mr. Williams says there are twenty sixpences in this little bit of money."

"Dear me!" said the gentleman; "is it possible? could I have done such a thing?" and he began to fumble in his waistcoat pocket.

"Well, really it is true enough," he added, as he drew out a sixpence. "See what it is to put gold and silver together."

"I wish he would give it to me," thought the little flower-girl; "how happy it would make poor granny; and perhaps he has got a good many more of these pretty gold pieces."

But the old gentleman put out his hand, and took it, and turned it over and over, and seemed to think a little; and then he put his hand into his pocket again, and took out his purse; and he put the half- sovereign into the purse, and took out of it another sixpence.

"Well," he said, "there is the sixpence I owe you for the flowers; you have done right to bring me back this piece of gold; and there is another sixpence for your race; it is not a reward, mind, for honesty is only our duty, and you only did what is right;

but you are tired, and have left your employment, and perhaps lost a customer, so I give you the other sixpence to make you amends."

"Thank you, sir," said the flower-girl, curtseying; and taking the two sixpences into her hand with a delighted smile, was going to run back again, when the old gentleman, pulling out a pocket-book, said, "Stay a moment; you are an orphan, they tell me; what is your name?"

"Fanny, sir."

"Fanny what?"

"Please, I don't know, sir; grandmother is Mrs. Newton, sir; but she says she is not my grandmother either, sir."

"Well, tell me where Mrs. Newton lives," said the gentleman, after looking at her a minute or so, as if trying to make out what she meant.

So Fanny told him, and he wrote it down in his pocket-book, and then read over what he had written to her, and she said it was right.

"Now, then, run away back," said he, "and sell all your flowers, if you can, before they wither, for they will not last long this warm day; flowers are like youth and beauty--do you ever think of that? even the rose withereth afore it groweth up." And this fat gentleman looked very sad, for he had lost all his children in their youth.

"O yes! sir; I know a verse which says that," replied Fanny. "All flesh is grass, and all the goodliness thereof is as the flower of grass--but good morning, and thank you, sir," and away Fanny ran.

And now, before going on with my story, I must go back to tell who and what Fanny, the flower-girl, was.

Mrs. Newton, whom she called her grandmother, was now a poor old woman, confined to her bed by a long and trying illness, that had nearly deprived her of the use of her limbs. But she had not been always thus afflicted. Some years before, Mrs. Newton lived in a neat cottage near the road-side, two or three miles from one of the great sea-port towns of England. Her husband had good employment, and they were both comfortable and happy.

Just eight years from this time, it happened that one warm summer's day, Mrs. Newton went to look out from her cottage door down the road, and she saw a young woman standing there, leaning against a tree, and looking very faint and weak.

She was touched with pity and asked the poor traveller to walk into her house and rest. The young woman thankfully consented, for she said she was very ill; but she added, that her husband was coming after her, having been obliged to turn back for a parcel that was left behind at the house where they had halted some time before, and therefore she would sit near the door and watch for him.

Before, however, the husband came, the poor woman was taken dreadfully ill; and when he did arrive, good Mrs. Newton could not bear to put the poor creature out of the house in such a state; she became worse and worse. In short, that poor young woman was Fanny's mother, and when little Fanny was born, that poor sick mother died, and Fanny never saw a mother's smile.

The day after the young woman's death, kind Mrs. Newton came into the room where her cold body was laid out on the bed; and there was her husband, a young, strong-looking man, sitting beside it; his elbows were on his knees, and his face was hid in his open hands.

Mrs. Newton had the baby in her arms, and she spoke to its father as she came in; he looked up to her; his own face was as pale as death; and he looked at her without saying a word. She saw he was in too much grief either to speak or weep. So she went over silently to him, and put the little baby into his arms, and then said, "May the Lord look down with pity on you both."

As soon as the unhappy young man heard these compassionate words, and saw the face of his pretty, peaceful babe, he burst into tears; they rolled in large drops down on the infant's head.

Then in a short time he was able to speak, and he told Mrs. Newton his sad little history; how he had no one in the whole world to look with pity on him, or his motherless child; and how God alone was his hope in this day of calamity. His father had been displeased with him because he had married that young woman, whom he dearly loved; and he had given him some money that was his portion, and would do nothing else for him. The young man had taken some land and a house, but as the rent was too high, he could not make enough of the land to pay it; so he had been obliged to sell all his goods, and he had only as much money left as would, with great saving, carry him to America, where he had a brother who advised him to go out there.

"And now," said he, looking over at the pale face of his dear wife, "What shall I do with the little creature she has left me? how shall I carry it over the wide ocean without a mother to care for it, and nurse it?"

"You cannot do so," said Mrs. Newton, wiping her eyes; "leave it with me; I have no children of my own, my husband would like to have one; this babe shall lie in my bosom, and be unto me as a daughter. I will nurse it for you until you are settled in America, and send or come for it."

The young man wept with gratitude; he wanted to know how he was to repay Mrs. Newton, but she said for the present she did not want payment, that it would be a pleasure to her to have the baby; and it would be time enough to talk about payment when the father was able to claim it, and take it to a home.

So the next day they buried the poor young woman, and soon after the young man went away and sailed off to America, and from that day to this Mrs. Newton had never heard anything of him.

As she had said, that poor little motherless babe lay in her bosom, and was unto her as a daughter; she loved it; she loved it when it was a helpless little thing, weak and sickly; she loved it when it grew a pretty lively baby, and would set its little feet on her knees, and crow and caper before her face; she loved it when it began to play around her as she sat at work, to lisp out the word "Ganny," for she taught it to call her grandmother; she loved it when it would follow her into her nice garden, and pick a flower and carry it to her, as she sat in the little arbor; and she, holding the flower, would talk to it of God who made the flower, and made the bee that drew honey from the flower, and made the sun that caused the flower to grow, and the light that gave the flower its colors, and the rain that watered it, and the earth that nourished it. And she loved that child when it came back from the infant school, and climbed up on her lap, or stood with its hands behind its back, to repeat some pretty verses about flowers, or about the God who made them. That child was Fanny, the flower-girl; and ah! how little did good Mrs. Newton think she would be selling flowers in the streets to help to support her.

But it came to pass, that when Fanny was nearly six years old, Mrs. Newton's husband fell very ill; it was a very bad, and very expensive illness, for poor Mrs. Newton was so uneasy, she would sometimes have two doctors to see him; but all would not do; he died: and Mrs. Newton was left very poorly off.

In a short time she found she could not keep on her pretty cottage; she was obliged to leave it; and the church where she had gone every Sunday for so many years; and the church-yard where her husband was buried, and little Fanny's mother; and the infant school where Fanny learned so much; and the dear little garden, and the flowers that were Fanny's teachers and favorites. Oh! how sorry was poor Mrs. Newton. But even a little child can give comfort; and so little Fanny, perhaps without thinking to do so, did; for when Mrs. Newton for the last time sat out in her garden, and saw the setting sun go down, and told Fanny she was going to leave that pretty garden, where she had from infancy been taught to know God's works, the child looked very sad and thoughtful indeed, for some time; but afterwards coming up to her, said,

"But, grandmother, we shall not leave God, shall we? for you say God is everywhere, and He will be in London too."

And oh! how that thought consoled poor Mrs. Newton; she did not leave God,--God did not leave her.

So she left the abode of her younger years--the scene of her widowhood; and she went away to hire a poor lodging in the outlets of London; but her God was with her, and the child she had nursed in her prosperity was her comfort in adversity.

Matters, however, went no better when she lived with little Fanny in a poor lodging. She had only one friend in London, and she lived at a distance from her. Mrs. Newton fell ill; there was no one to nurse her but Fanny; she could no longer pay for her schooling, and sometimes she was not able to teach her herself.

All this seemed very hard, and very trying; and one would have been tempted to think that God was no longer with poor Mrs. Newton; that when she had left her cottage she had left the God who had been so good to her.

But this would have been a great mistake. God was with Mrs. Newton; He saw fit to try and afflict her; but He gave her strength and patience to bear her trials and afflictions.

One afternoon her friend came to pay her a visit: she was going out a little way into the country to see a relation who had a very fine nursery-garden, and she begged Mrs. Newton to let little Fanny go with her own daughter. Mrs. Newton was very glad to do so for she thought it would be a nice amusement for Fanny.

The nurseryman was very kind to her; and when she was going away gave her a fine bunch of flowers. Fanny was in great delight, for she loved flowers and knew her dear grandmother loved them too. But as she was coming back, and just as she was entering the streets, she met a lady and a little boy of about three years old, who directly held out his hands and began to beg for the flowers. His mamma stopped, and as Fanny was very poorly dressed, she thought it probable that she would sell her nosegay, and so she said,

"Will you give that bunch of flowers to my little boy, and I will pay you for it?"

"Please, ma'am, they are for grandmother," said Fanny blushing, and thinking she ought to give the flowers directly, and without money to any one who wished for them.

"But perhaps your grand-mother would rather have this sixpence?" said the lady. And Mrs. Newton's friend, who had just come up, said,

"Well, my dear, take the lady's sixpence, and let her have the flowers if she wishes for them."

So Fanny held the flowers to the lady, who took them and put the sixpence in her hand. Fanny wished much to ask for one rose, but she thought it would not be right to do so, when the lady had bought them all: and she looked at them so very longingly that the lady asked if she were sorry to part with them.

"Oh! no, ma'am," cried her friend, "she is not at all sorry--come now, don't be a fool, child," she whispered, and led Fanny on.

"That is a good bargain for you," she added as she went on; "that spoiled little master has his own way, I think; it would be well for you, and your grandmother too, if you could sell sixpenny worth of flowers every day."

"Do you think I could, ma'am?" said Fanny, opening her hand and looking at her sixpence, "this will buy something to do poor granny good; do you think Mr. Simpson would give me a nosegay every day?"

"If you were to pay him for it, he would," said her friend; "suppose you were to go every morning about five o'clock, as many others do, and buy some flowers, and then sell them at the market; you might earn something, and that would be better than being idle, when poor Mrs. Newton is not able to do for herself and you."

So when Fanny got back, she gave her dear grandmother the sixpence.

"The Lord be praised!" said Mrs. Newton, "for I scarcely knew how I was to get a loaf of bread for thee or myself to-morrow."

And then Fanny told her the plan she had formed about the flowers.

Mrs. Newton was very sorry to think her dear child should be obliged to stand in a market place, or in the public streets, to offer anything for sale; but she said, "Surely it is Providence has opened this means of gaining a little bread, while I am laid here unable to do anything; and shall I not trust that Providence with the care of my darling child?"

So from this time forth little Fanny set off every morning before five o'clock, to the nursery garden; and the nursery-man was very kind to her, and always gave her the nicest flowers; and instead of sitting down with the great girls, who went there also for flowers or vegetables, and tying them up in bunches, Fanny put them altogether in her little basket, and went away to her grandmother's room, and spread them out on the little table that poor Mrs. Newton might see them, while the sweet dew was yet sparkling on their bright leaves.

Then she would tell how beautiful the garden looked at that sweet early hour; and Mrs. Newton would listen with pleasure, for she loved a garden. She used to say, that God placed man in a garden when he was happy and holy; and when he was sinful and sorrowful, it was in a garden that the blessed Saviour wept and prayed for the sin of the world; and when his death had made atonement for that sin, it was in a garden his blessed body was laid.

Mrs. Newton taught Fanny many things from flowers; she was not a bad teacher, in her own simple way, but Jesus Christ, who was the best teacher the world ever had, instructed his disciples from vines and lilies, corn and fruit, and birds, and all natural things around them.

And while Fanny tied up her bunches of flowers, she would repeat some verses from the Holy Scriptures, such as this, "O Lord, how manifold are thy works! in wisdom hast thou made them all: the earth is full of thy riches." And afterwards she would repeat such pretty lines as these:--

"Not worlds on worlds, in varied form,
Need we, to tell a God is here;
The daisy, saved from winter's storm,
Speaks of his hand in lines as clear.

"For who but He who formed the skies,
And poured the day-spring's living flood,
Wondrous alike in all He tries,
Could rear the daisy's simple bud!

"Mould its green cup, its wiry stem,
Its fringed border nicely spin;
And cut the gold-embossed gem,
That, shrined in silver, shines within;

"And fling it, unrestrained and free,
O'er hill, and dale, and desert sod,
That man, where'er he walks, may see,
In every step the trace of God."

"And I, too, have had my daisy given to me," poor Mrs. Newton would say, with tearful eyes, as she gazed on her little flower-girl; "I too have my daisy, and though it may be little cared for in the world, or trodden under foot of men, yet will it ever bear, I trust, the trace of God."

But it happened the very morning that the gentleman had given Fanny the half-sovereign in mistake, Mrs. Newton's money was quite spent; and she was much troubled, thinking the child must go the next morning to the garden without money to pay for her flowers, for she did not think it likely she would sell enough to buy what they required, and pay for them also; so she told Fanny she must ask Mr. Simpson to let her owe him for a day or two until she got a little money she expected.

Fanny went therefore, and said this to the kind man at the garden; and he put his hand on her head, and said, "My pretty little girl, you may owe me as long as you please, for you are a good child, and God will prosper you."

So Fanny went back in great delight, and told this to Mrs. Newton; and to cheer her still more, she chose for her morning verse, the advice that our Lord gave to all those who were careful and troubled about the things of this life "Consider the lilies of the field, how they grow; they toil not, neither do they spin; and yet I say unto you that Solomon in all his glory, was not arrayed like one of these. Wherefore, if God so clothe the grass of the field, which to-day is, and to-morrow is cast into the oven, shall he not much more clothe you, oh ye of little faith?"

And then she repeated some verses which both she and Mrs. Newton liked very much.

"Lo! the lilies of the field,
How their leaves instruction yield!
Hark to nature's lesson, given
By the blessed birds of heaven.

"Say with richer crimson glows,
The kingly mantle than the rose;
Say are kings more richly dressed,
Than the lily's glowing vest!

"Grandmother I forget the next verse," said Fanny, interrupting herself; "I know it is something about lilies not spinning; but then comes this verse--

"Barns, nor hoarded store have we"--

"It is not the lilies, grandmother, but the blessed birds that are speaking now--

"Barns, nor hoarded store have we,
Yet we carol joyously;
Mortals, fly from doubt and sorrow,
God provideth for the morrow."

Poor Mrs. Newton clasped her thin hands, and looked up, and prayed like the disciples, "Lord, increase our faith!"

"Eh!" said she, afterwards, "is it not strange that we can trust our Lord and Saviour with the care of our souls for eternity, and we cannot trust Him with that of our bodies for a day."

Well! this was poor Mrs. Newton's state on that day, when the gentleman gave Fanny the half-sovereign instead of sixpence, for her flowers.

When the little flower-girl came back from her race with her two sixpences, she found the old vegetable-seller had got her three or four pennies more, by merely showing her basket, and telling why it was left at his stall; and so every one left a penny for the honest child, and hoped the gentleman would reward her well. The old man at the stall said it was very shabby of him only to give her sixpence; but when she went home with three sixpences and told Mrs. Newton this story, she kissed her little girl very fondly, but said the gentleman was good to give her sixpence, for he had no right to give her anything, she had only done her duty.

"But, grandmother," said Fanny, "when I saw that pretty half- sovereign dropping down to his purse, I could not help wishing he would give it to me."

"And what commandment did you break then, my child?"

"Not the eighth--if I had kept the half-sovereign I should have broken it," said Fanny, "for that says, thou shalt not steal--what commandment did I break, grandmother; for I did not steal?"

"When we desire to have what is not ours Fanny, what do we do? we covet; do we not?"

"Oh! yes--thou shalt not covet thy neighbor's goods," cried Fanny, "that is the tenth commandment; and that half-sovereign was my neighbor's goods, and that fat gentleman was my neighbor. But, grandmother, it is very easy to break the tenth commandment."

"Very easy indeed, my dear," said Mrs. Newton, with first a faint smile, and then a deep sigh, "therefore," she added, "we ought always to pray like David, 'Turn away mine eyes from beholding vanity.'"

There is a very common saying, that when things are at the worst they mend. It is hard to say when matters are at the worst; poor Mrs. Newton knew they might yet be worse with her; but certainly, they were very bad; and a few days after this, as Fanny was tying up her flowers as usual, she lay on her bed thinking what she was to do, and praying that God would direct her to some way of providing for the poor child.

While she was thinking and praying, tears stole down her face; Fanny saw them, and stopped her work, and looked sorrowfully at her--

"Now you are crying again, grandmother, she said," and that's what makes me break the tenth commandment, for I can't help wishing the gentleman had given me that half-sovereign. But I will say the verses again to-day about the lilies and birds; for you know I said that morning--

'Mortals fly from doubt and sorrow,
God provideth for the morrow,'

and when I came back with my three sixpences, you said God **had** provided for the morrow, for you had only two or three pennies in the house when I went out."

"And how many pennies, pray, have you in the house to-day?" said a rather gruff voice at the door.

Mrs. Newton and Fanny started; but there, standing at the door, Fanny saw the fat gentleman who had given her the half-sovereign.

"So you have been wishing for my gold, you little rogue," he said, looking as if he meant to frighten her. "Never mind," he added, smiling, "you are a good child, and did what was right; and I always meant to bring it back to you, but I have been kept rather busy these few days past. There it is for you, and try not to break the tenth commandment again." Then turning to Mrs. Newton, he said, "We should not expect rewards, ma'am, for doing our duty, but if children do not meet with approbation when they do right, they may be discouraged, and perhaps think there is no use in being good: for they are silly little creatures, you know, and do not always recollect that God will reward the just one day if men do not."

"Oh! sir!" said poor Mrs. Newton, but the tears streamed down, and she could not say a word more. And there Fanny sat gazing on the half- sovereign, as if she was half stupefied.

"Well, take up that bit of gold, and do what you like with it," said the fat gentleman; "and then run off to sell your flowers, for we must not be idle because we have got enough for to-day. But do what you like with that money."

Fanny rose up from her seat, and looking very much as if she was moving in her sleep, with her wondering eyes fixed on the shining piece that lay in her hand, she walked slowly over to Mrs. Newton, and putting it into hers, said,--

"May I go to the grocer's now, grandmother, and get you the tea for your breakfast?"

"Yes, my love," said Mrs. Newton, kissing her, "and take care of this, and bring back the change carefully." Then turning to the gentleman, she said, "I am not young, sir, and I am very, very poorly; I find it hard to go without my tea, but it is a luxury I have been obliged latterly to forego."

"But could you not get tea on credit, from the grocer?" said the gentleman.

"Oh! yes, I believe so; but there would be no use in getting credit;" said Mrs. Newton, "for I am not certain of being better able to pay next week than I am this week; and when I have not the money to pay for what I wish to get, it is better to do without it, than to add to one's anxieties by running in debt. Do you not think so, sir?"

"Ma'am," said the old gentleman, sitting down, and resting his large silver-topped stick between his knees, "it is of very little consequence what I think; but if you wish to know this, I will tell you that I think very well both of you and your little girl, who, as I have heard, for I have made inquiries about you both, is a dependant on your bounty. You have trained her up well, though I wouldn't praise the child to her face; and so take as much tea as you like till you hear from me again, and your grocer need be in no trouble about his bill."

So after the fat gentleman had made this rather bluff, but honest- hearted speech, and poor Mrs. Newton had wept, and thanked him in language that sounded more polite, the good old gentleman told her his whole history.

He began the world very poor, and without relations able to assist him; he was at last taken into the employment of a young merchant in the city; he had a turn for business, and having been able to render some important services to this young man, he was finally, to his own surprise, and that of every one else, taken into partnership.

"During all this time," said he, "I was attached from my boyhood to the daughter of the poor schoolmaster who first taught me to read; I would not marry her while I was poor, for I thought that would be to make her wretched instead of happy; but when I was taken into partnership I thought my way was clear; I went off to Bethnal Green, and told Mary, and our wedding-day was settled at once. Well, we were glad enough, to be sure; but a very few days after, my partner called me into the private room, and said he wanted to consult me. He seemed in high spirits, and he told me he had just heard of a famous speculation, by which we could both make our fortunes at once. He explained what it was, and I saw with shame and regret, that no really honest man could join in it: I told him so; I told him plainly I would have nothing to do with it. You may think what followed; the deeds of partnership were not yet signed, and in short, in two or three days more I found myself poor

Jack Walton again--indeed, poorer than I was before I was made one of the firm of Charters and Walton, for I had lost my employment.

"Often and often I used to think that David said, he had never seen the righteous forsaken; yet I was suffering while the unrighteous were prospering. It was a sinful, and a self-righteous thought, and I was obliged to renounce it; when, after some time of trial, a gentleman sent for me--a man of wealth, and told me his son was going into business on his own account; that he had heard of my character, and of the cause of my leaving Mr. Charters; that he thought I would be just such a steady person as he wished his son to be with. In short, I began with him on a handsome salary; was soon made his partner; married Mary, and had my snug house in the country. Mr. Charters succeeded in that speculation; entered into several others, some of which were of a more fraudulent nature, failed, and was ruined. He ran off to America, and no one knows what became of him. I have left business some years. I purchased a nice property in the country, built a Church upon it, and have ever thanked God, who never forsakes those who wish to act righteously.

"It pleased God to take all my sweet children from me--every state has its trials--the youngest was just like your little flower-girl."

Mrs. Newton was much pleased with this story; she then told her own, and little Fanny's. The fat gentleman's eyes were full of tears when she ended; when he was going away he put another half-sovereign into her hand, and saying, "The first was for the child," walked out of the house.

A short time afterwards, a clergyman came to see Mrs. Newton--she was surprised; he sat and talked with her some time, and seemed greatly pleased with her sentiments, and all she told him of herself and Fanny. He then told her that he was the clergyman whom Mr. Walton, on the recommendation of the bishop of the diocese, had appointed to the church he had built; that Mr. Walton had sent him to see her, and had told him, if he was satisfied with all he saw and heard, to invite Mrs. Newton and the little flower-girl to leave London, and go and live in one of the nice widows' houses, which good Mr. Walton had built, near the pretty village where he lived.

Then there was great joy in poor Mrs. Newton's humble abode; Mrs. Newton was glad for Fanny's sake, and Fanny was glad for Mrs. Newton's sake, so both were glad, and both said--

"Mortals fly from doubt and sorrow,
God provideth for the morrow."

But the only difference was, that Mrs. Newton said it with watery eyes and clasped hands, lying on her bed and looking up to heaven; and Fanny--merry little thing!--said it frisking and jumping about the room, clapping her hands together, and laughing her joy aloud.

Well, there was an inside place taken in the B---- coach, for Mrs. Newton and Fanny; and not only that, but kind Mrs. Walton sent up her own maid to London, to see that everything was carefully done, as the poor woman was ill, and help to pack up all her little goods; and, with her, she sent an entire new suit of clothes for the flower-girl.

They set off, and when they got near to the village the coachman stopped, and called out to know if it were the first, or the last of the red cottages he was to stop at; and Mrs. Walton's maid said, "The last,--the cottage in the garden." So they stopped at such a pretty cottage, with a little garden before and behind it. Mr. Walton had known what it was to be poor, and so, when he grew rich, he had built these neat houses, for those who had been rich and become poor. They were intended chiefly for the widows of men of business, whose character had been good, but who had died without being able to provide for their families. He had made an exception in Mrs. Newton's case, and gave her one of the best houses, because it had a pretty garden, which he thought others might not care for so much.

They went inside, and there was such a neat kitchen, with tiles as red as tiles could be; a little dresser, with all sorts of useful things; a nice clock ticking opposite the fire-place, and a grate as bright as blacklead could make it. And then there was such a pretty little room at one side, with a rose tree against the window; and a little shelf for books against the wall; and a round table, and some chairs, and an easy couch. And there were two nice bedrooms overhead; and, better than all these, was a pretty garden. Oh! how happy was the little flower-girl; and how thankful was poor Mrs. Newton! The first thing she did was to go down on her knees and thank God.

Then Fanny was to go to the school, for Mrs. Walton had her own school, as well as the national school; but Fanny did not know enough to go to it, so she was sent to the national school first, and afterwards she went to the other, where about a dozen girls were instructed in all things that would be useful to them through life-- whether they were to earn their bread at service, or to live in their own homes as daughters, wives, or mothers.

But every morning, before she went out, she did everything for her dear, good grandmother. She made her breakfast; she arranged her room; and she gathered some fresh flowers in the garden, and put them on the table in the little parlor. Oh! how happy was Fanny when she looked back, and saw how nice everything looked, and then went out singing to her school--

"Barns, nor hoarded store have we,
Yet we carol joyously;
Mortals flee from doubt and sorrow,
God provideth for the morrow."

But God will not provide for the morrow, where people will do nothing to provide for themselves; and so Fanny, the flower-girl, knew, for surely God had blessed the labor of her childish hands.

Thus passed time away; and Fanny, under the instruction that she had at church, at school, and at home, "grew in grace, and in the knowledge and love of God, and of Jesus Christ our Lord."

Good Mrs. Newton was much better in health, and used to walk about sometimes without any support but Fanny's arm, and so time went on till Fanny came to be about fifteen; and then Mrs. Newton, who was not always free from "doubt and sorrow," began to think what was to become of her if she were to die.

So one day, when kind Mr. Walton, whom Fanny used once to call the fat gentleman, came in to see her, Mrs. Newton told him that she was beginning to feel anxious that Fanny should be put in a way of earning her own bread, in case she should be taken from her.

Mr. Walton listened to her, and then he said,--

"You are very right and prudent, Mrs. Newton, but never mind that; I have not forgotten my little flower-girl, and her race after me that hot morning; if you were dead, I would take care of her; and if we both were dead, Mrs. Walton would take care of her; and if Mrs. Walton were dead, God would take care of her. I see you cannot yet learn the little lines she is so fond of--

"'Mortals flee from doubt and sorrow,
God provideth for the morrow.'"

Well, not very long after this conversation came a very warm day, and in all the heat of the sun came Mr. Walton, scarcely able to breathe, into Mrs. Newton's cottage; he was carrying his hat in one hand, and a newspaper in the other, and his face was very red and hot.

"Well, Mrs. Newton," said he, "what is all this about?--I can't make it out; here is your name in the paper!"

"My name, sir!" said Mrs. Newton, staring at the paper.

"Aye, indeed is it," said Mr. Walton, putting on his spectacles, and opening the paper at the advertisement side,--"see here!"

And he began to read,--

"If Mrs. Newton, who lived about fifteen years ago near the turnpike on the P-- road, will apply to Messrs. Long and Black, she will hear of something to her advantage. Or should she be dead, any person who can give information respecting her and her family, will be rewarded."

Mrs. Newton sat without the power of speech--so much was she surprised; at last she said, "It is Fanny's father!--I know, I am sure it can be no one else!"

Mr. Walton looked surprised, for he had never thought of this; he was almost sorry to think his little flower-girl should have another protector. At length he said it must be as Mrs. Newton thought, and he would go up to London himself next day, and see Mr. Long and Mr. Black. So he went; and two days afterwards, when Fanny had returned from Mrs. Walton's school, and was sitting with Mrs. Newton in the little shady arbor they had made in the garden, and talking over early days, when they used to sit in another arbor, and Fanny used to learn her first lessons from flowers, then came Mr. Walton walking up the path towards them, and with him was a fine-looking man, of about forty-five years of age.

Mrs. Newton trembled, for when she looked in his face she remembered the features; and she said to herself, "Now, if he takes my Fanny from me?--and if he should be a bad man?" But when this man came nearer, he stepped hastily beyond Mr. Walton, and catching Mrs. Newton's hands, he was just going to drop on his knees before her, when he saw Fanny staring at him; and a father's feelings overcame every other, and with a cry of joy he extended his arms, and exclaiming "my child!'--my child!" caught her to his breast.

Then there followed so much talk, while no one knew scarcely what was saying; and it was Mr. Walton, chiefly, that told how Fanny's father had had so much to struggle against, and so much hardship to go through, but how he had succeeded at last, and got on very well; now he had tried then to find out Mrs. Newton and his dear little Fanny, but could not, because Mrs. Newton had changed her abode; how, at last, he had met with a good opportunity to sell his land, and had now come over with the money he had earned, to find his child, and repay her kind benefactor.

Oh, what a happy evening was that in the widow's cottage! the widow's heart sang for joy. The widow, and she that had always thought herself an orphan, were ready to sing together--

"Mortals flee from doubt and sorrow,
God provideth for the morrow."

Mrs. Newton found that Mr. Marsden, that was the name of Fanny's father, was all that she could desire Fanny's father to be:--a Christian in deed and in truth; one thankful to God and to her, for the preservation and care of his child; and who would not willingly separate Fanny from her, or let her leave Fanny.

As he found Mrs. Newton did not wish to leave kind Mr. Walton's neighborhood, and that his daughter was attached to it also, Mr. Marsden took some land and a nice farm-house, not far from the Manor House, where Mr. Walton lived. He had heard all about the half- sovereign, and loved his little flower-girl before he saw her.

So Mrs. Newton had to leave her widow's house; and she shed tears of joy, and regret, and thankfulness, as she did so; she had been happy there, and had had God's blessing upon her and her dear girl.

But Fanny was glad to receive her dear, dear grandmother into her own father's house; her own house too; and she threw her arms round the old lady's neck, when they got there, and kissed her over and over again, and said, "Ah! grandmother, do you recollect when I was a little girl tying up my flowers while you lay sick in bed, I used to say so often--

"'Mortals flee from doubt and sorrow,
God provideth for the morrow.'"

They had a large garden at the farm-house, and Fanny and Mrs. Newton improved it; and Mrs. Newton would walk out, leaning on Fanny's arm, and look at the lilies and roses, and jessamine, and mignonette, and talk of past times, and of their first garden, and their first flowers, and of their first knowledge of the God who made them; who watches the opening bud, and the infant head; who sends his rain upon the plant, and the dew of his blessing upon the child who is taught to know and love Him. And Fanny's father, when he joined them, talked over his trials and dangers from the day that his poor wife lay dead, and his helpless baby lay in his arms, and then he blessed the God who had led him all his life long, and crowned him with loving- kindness.

Three years passed, and Fanny, the little flower-girl, was a fine young woman. A farmer's son in the neighborhood wished to get her for his wife; but her father was very sorry to think of her leaving him so soon for another home.

He spoke to Fanny about it, and said,--"My dear girl, I have no right to expect you should wish to stay with me, for I never was able to watch over your childhood or to act a father's part by you."

And Fanny answered, with a blush and smile, "And I, father, was never able to act a daughter's part by you until now, and therefore I think you have every right to expect I should do so for some time longer. I have no objections to be Charles Brierley's wife, and I have told him so; but we are both young, and at all events I will not leave you."

"Now," said Mrs. Newton, who was sitting by, "instead of that young man taking more land, which is very dear about here, would it not be a good plan if he were to come and live with you, Mr. Marsden, and help you with the farm."

And Mr. Marsden said, "That is the very thing; I will go and speak to him about it; and Fanny and her husband can have the house, and farm, and all, as much as they please now, and entirely at my death."

So it was all settled; and Fanny was married at the village church, and Mr. and Mrs. Walton were at the wedding. Good Mrs. Newton lived on at the farm-house, and when Fanny's first child was born, it was put into her arms. Then she thought of the time when Fanny herself was laid in the same arms; and she blessed God in her heart, who had enabled her to be of use to one human creature, and to one immortal soul and mind, while she passed through this life to the life everlasting.

Joy and sorrow are always mingled on this earth; so it came to pass that before Fanny's first child could walk alone, good, kind Mrs. Newton died, and was buried. As a shock of corn cometh in, in its season, so she sank to rest, and was gathered into the garner of her Lord. But--

"The memory of the just
Is blessed, though they sleep in dust;"

and Fanny's children, and children's children, will learn to love that memory.

Many a day, sitting at work in her garden, with her little ones around her, Fanny let them gather some flowers, and talk to her about them; and then they would beg, as a reward for good conduct, that she would tell them about her dear grandmother and her own childish days; and much as children love to hear stories, never did any more delight in a story, than did these children, in the story of Fanny, the Flower-Girl.

Convenient Food.

Little Frances was crying; her sister Mary hearing her sobs, ran in haste to inquire what had happened; and saw her sitting in a corner of the nursery, looking rather sulky, as if she had recently received some disappointment.

"What is the matter, dear little Frances? why do you cry so?"

Frances pouted, and would make no reply.

"Tell me, dear Frances; perhaps I can do something for you."

"Nothing, Mary," she sobbed, "only"--

"Only what, little Frances? It cannot be ***nothing*** that makes you cry so bitterly."

"Only mamma would not give--" she looked a little ashamed, and did not finish her sentence.

"***What*** would she not give?"

"Nothing."

"Nothing!" Frances shook her elbows, as if troubled by Mary's inquiries, but the tears continued flowing down her cheeks.

Just at that moment their sister Anne came into the room, singing in the joy of her heart, with a piece of plum-cake in her hand, holding it up, and turning it about before her sisters to exhibit her newly-acquired possession, on which Frances fixed her eyes with eager gaze, and the tears flowed still faster, accompanied with a kind of angry sob.

"Frances! what is the matter that you are crying so? see what I have got! you will spoil all the happiness of our feast."

At the word *feast*, Frances' tears seemed arrested, and her mouth looked as if she were going to smile. She left the corner, and immediately prepared to do her part for the feast, setting a little square table, and then, drawing her own little stool, seated herself in readiness as a guest.

"Stay," said Anne, "we will make some little paper dishes and plates, and divide the cake;" so saying, she began the operation, and laying down the paper dishes, "there at the top, see! there shall be two chickens, at the bottom a piece of beef, at one side some potatoes, and at the other some cauliflower;" breaking her cake into small pieces to correspond to her imagined provision.

Frances looked very impatient at the long preparation, and as Anne seated herself, inviting Mary to partake, Frances stretched out her hand to take the beef for her own portion.

"No, no, Frances, you must not help yourself, you know; wait until we all begin in order."

Frances very reluctantly withdrew her hand, and, whilst she waited, betrayed her impatience by a little jerking motion of the body, that threw her breast against the table, as if she would beat time into quicker motion.

"O we must not forget William!" Anne exclaimed; "where is he? he must taste our feast; stay here, Mary, with Frances, and I will go and find him."

Away she ran, and left poor Frances in a fret at this additional delay, but she began to amuse herself by picking up the small crumbs that had been scattered on the stool, and at last proceeded to touch the beef and chickens.

"Do not do so, Frances," Mary said, in a reproving voice.

Frances colored.

"Do not sit *looking* on, if you are so impatient; employ yourself, and get a seat ready for William."

"*You* may get it, Mary."

"Very well; only do not meddle with Anne's feast."

Mary had to go into another room for the seat, and whilst she was away, Frances quickly helped herself to half of the pieces which were on the dishes, and, when Mary returned, resumed her position as if nothing had happened. Mary was so busy in arranging the seats, that she did not observe what had been done.

Presently Anne came back, accompanied by her brother William; hastening to her place, and looking on her table, she started with surprise, and seemed to say to herself, as she gazed, How came I to make a mistake, an think my pieces of cake were larger? but the expression of her face called Mary's attention, who at once said,

"Anne, I am sure you placed larger pieces on your dishes."

"Indeed, I thought so, Mary; who has taken any?"

"I do not know."

"O you are only *pretending*, and you have been hiding some."

"No, Anne; I would not have said I do not know, if I had *hid* it."

"No, no more you would, dear Mary. Never mind," she said, glancing a look at Frances, not altogether without suspicion, "it is only to *play* with, it does not signify whether it is much or little.

"William, shall I help you to a little chicken?"

"O no, Anne, you have forgot, help the *ladies* first; and beside, you ought to have placed me at the bottom of the table to carve this dish. What is it?"

"Beef, William."

"O beef, very well. Come, Miss Frances, let me sit there, and you come to the side of the table."

In haste to begin the eating part of the play, she rose immediately to change places, when, to her disgrace, a quantity of crumbs, which had lodged unobserved in a fold of her frock, fell out, and disordered the neatness of the table.

"There!" said William, "we have no question to ask who took the liberty to lessen the dishes."

"For shame, William, I--"

"O Frances, take care what you say, tell no falsehoods; I will tell one truth, and say you are a greedy girl."

Frances began to cry again, "For shame, William, to call me names."

"I call no names, I only say what I think, and how can I help it, when it is only just now you cried so, because you said mamma had given me a larger piece of cake than yourself; for you must know," he continued, turning to Mary, "we have both had one piece before, and she half of mine to make her quiet; and then she cried again because a piece was put by for you and Anne, and she cannot be contented now, though Anne shares hers amongst us. If this is not being greedy, I do not know what greedy means. It is no names, it is only saying what a thing is."

"Now I know another thing," said Anne; "when mamma called me to receive my piece of cake, she said, 'And you shall take a piece also to Mary,' but when she unfolded the paper, there was only *one* piece; mamma did not say anything, but I think she *thought* something."

At this remark, Frances redoubled her crying, but, for the sake of a share of the present feast, did not attempt to leave the party. No more was said, and the feast was concluded in good humor by all except the conscious greedy girl, and they then all went into the garden together to finish their hour's recreation before they were called again to their lessons.

There was a little plantation of young fir-trees at one corner of the garden, intended to grow there for shelter from the north-west wind: the grass was so high amongst them, that the gardener had orders to go and carefully mow it down. He was engaged in the business when the children ran out to see him work.

"Hush! hush!" he exclaimed, as they approached, "I have just cleared a bough from the grass, and see what's there!"

All curiosity, they went forward on tip-toe, and were directed to something lodged on the spreading branch of a young larch.

"A bird's nest!" said William.

"A bird's nest!" they all repeated. "But what is in it, I cannot tell."

"Look steadily," said the gardener, "and you will find out."

It was difficult to trace what it was; something all in a heap, brown naked skin; alive, as might be known by the heaving breathing. William putting his finger to touch them, immediately four wide mouths stretched open, with little tongues raised, and the opening of their throats extended to the utmost.

"Look at the little things," said William; "they thought their mother was come when I touched the branch, and they have opened their mouths to be ready to receive what she would put in.

"They are **blind**!" said William.

"Yes, they cannot have been hatched more than two days."

"Will they take what the mother gives them?" asked William.

"Yes," said the man, "they trust her, and swallow down what she puts into their mouths."

"I wish the mother would come," said Anne.

"But she will not whilst we are here," William replied.

"Touch it again, William," said Frances.

William touched the edge of the nest "See!" said he, "they think the mother is come, they stretch, their months still wider."

"Hark!" said Mary, "what an impatient noise they make: they look ready to stretch themselves out of their nest, and as if their little mouths would tear."

"Poor little things! do not disappoint them, give them something," said Anne.

"We have not proper food for them," said William.

"I will run and fetch some crumbs," said Mary.

Mary soon returned with a piece of bread, and giving it to her brother as the most experienced, he broke it into extremely small crumbs, and, again touching the nest, awakened the expectation of the young birds: they opened their mouths wide, and as he dropped a small crumb into each, they moved their tongues, trying to make it pass down into their throat. "Poor little things, they cannot swallow well, they want the mother to put it gently down their throat with her beak."

"See! see!" said all the girls, "they want more, give them more."

William dropped his crumbs again.

"More, more, William; see! they are not satisfied."

"I dare not give them more for fear of killing them, we cannot feed them like the mother. We will stand still at a little distance, and you will see them go to sleep." When all was quiet, the little nestlings shut their mouths, and dropped their heads.

"I should like to see the mother feed them."

"You would see how much better she would do it than we can; perhaps, if we could conceal ourselves behind that laurel, she would come, but she will be very frightened, because all is so altered now the grass is cut down, and her nest is exposed; but I dare say she is not for off, she will be watching somewhere."

They took William's hint, and retreated behind the laurel; they had not waited ten minutes, before the hen bird flitted past, and, darting over the larch, as if to inspect whether her little brood was safe, she disappeared again. In a few minutes more, she returned, skimming round to reconnoitre that all was safe, she perched upon the nest. Instantly the little nestlings were awake to the summons of her touch and chirp, and, opening their mouths wide, were ready for what she would give. She dropt a small fly into the mouth of one of them, and, having no more, flew away to provide for the other hungry mouths as fast as she could. As soon as she was gone, they again shut their mouths, and dropt their heads in silence.

"What a little bit she gave them," said Frances.

"Yes," answered William, "but she knows it is ***plenty***."

"How contented the others seem to wait till she comes again!"

"Yes, Mary," William again answered, unable to resist the comparison which had come to his mind, "they did not take the little bit away from the other. Shall we wait till she comes again?"

"O do."

"Very well, I want to see whether the one that was fed first will take away the bit the others got."

The allusion made a little laugh, but, seeing that Frances understood and felt that it applied to her, Anne said, "Do not let us tease Frances; it is better to tell her at once what her fault is, than to seem to like to hurt her."

"Indeed, dear Anne, I have not spared to tell her, her fault, as she knows very well, for she has often given me reason, but I cannot make her ashamed of such things; and I know mamma is very uneasy to see it in her."

Frances looked grave, but did not cry; turning pale, however, she said, "O Mary take me out of this laurel--I am so sick!"

Mary hastened to take her into the freer air, but all in vain. The sisters were alarmed, and took her in to their mamma; who received her gravely, without expressing any concern for her indisposition.

"What can we do for Frances, mamma? Will you let her have your smelling bottle, or shall I run and get some sal volatile?"

"Neither, my dear Mary; it is an indisposition caused by her own selfish appetite, and probably the relief may be obtained by her stomach rejecting what she so improperly forced upon it. We will wait a short time, and if not, I will give her something less palatable, perhaps, than plum-cake, but necessary to remove it."

Frances was too ill to make any remark; she became paler still, and then quickly flushed almost a crimson color, her eyes were oppressed, and her eyebrows contracted, and she impatiently complained,

"O my head! how it beats! What shall I do, mamma?"

"Bear the consequences of your own inordinate appetite, Frances, and learn to subject it to the wholesome rules of temperance."

"O the nasty plum-cake! I wish you had not given me any, mamma."

"You **once** thought the plum-cake **nice**, and you would not be contented with the small portion I knew to be sufficient and safe for you."

"O my head! I think it is very cruel, mamma, that you do not pity me."

"I do pity you, Frances, and will take care of you now that I see you require help, as I perceive that you will not have any relief without medicine."

Frances began again to cry, "O, I am so sick! I cannot take medicine. I am sure I cannot."

"Come to your room, Frances; I shall give you something proper, and you had better lie down after you have taken it; you will, perhaps, drop into a sleep, and be well when you awake again." Her mamma took her hand and led her up stairs, and Frances knew very well it was in vain to make any objection, as her mamma always made a point of obedience. The medicine was administered, although for some time Frances refused to look at it. When she laid down, her mamma placed the pillow high under her head, and, drawing the curtain to shade the light, left the room that she might be perfectly quiet. And when she returned to the drawing-room, she inquired of the other children what they had been doing, and received a full account of the feast, and the bird's nest, and all the little circumstances of each.

It was time to resume their studies, and, except that Frances was not in her usual place, all things proceeded as before. When the lessons were finished, they entreated their mamma to go with them, and see the bird's nest."

"It is *so* pretty, mamma!" said Anne; "and they know when the mother comes, and they take what she puts into their mouths."

"We will first inquire after Frances," she answered; "if she is well enough, she can accompany us."

"I will run up, if you will be putting on your bonnet and shawl, mamma."

"Very well, I hope you will find her recovered, we will wait your return."

Anne soon returned,--"She is gone! I do not see her anywhere!"

"Gone! In perhaps we shall find her at play in the garden."

In this expectation they all went out, and as they drew near the spot where the nest was, they saw Frances looking very eagerly into the nest, and seeming to be in some agitation, then she threw something out of her hand, and ran away as if wanting not to be seen.

"She is about some mischief," William said, and ran forward to the nest. But what was his grief to see one of the little birds dead on the ground, two others in the nest with pieces of bread sticking in their mouths, gasping, unable to swallow or reject it, and the fourth with its crop gorged, and slowly moving its little unfledged head from side to side, struggling in death.

Full of sympathy with the little sufferer, and indignant with Frances, he exclaimed, "Provoking girl! she has stuffed the little creatures as she would like to stuff herself; and I believe she has killed them all."

The lively interest the other children had in the nest, impelled them to hasten to the spot, and their lamentations, and even tears, soon flowed.

"William, William, cannot you do anything for them? do try."

"Well, stand still and do not shake my arm--so saying, he began the attempt, and drew the bread carefully out of the distended mouths of the two.

"Now the other! the other, William!"

"That I cannot help," he answered: "see! she has forced it down, and we cannot get it back again; it is dying now."

Anne picked up the dead one from off the ground, and stroking it with her forefinger, "Poor little thing!" she said, "was she so cruel to you!"

It was not long before they heard a rustling in the tree near the place, and then a chirp of fright and distress. "Ah!" said their mamma, "there is the mother! poor things, we will go a little distance to let her come to the nest; perhaps she will be able to save the two."

They all withdrew, and the little parent bird was soon on her nest, fluttering and chirping to awaken the dead and dying little ones, till at length she sorrowfully brooded down on her nest, and spread her wings over them, occasionally chirping as if to solicit an answer from her little brood.

"Oh!" said Mary, bursting into tears, "I cannot bear it! cruel Frances, to be so unkind to the little birds!"

"Go and find Frances," said their mamma, "and bring her to me."

"I will go," William answered, "I think I know where she will hide herself."

It was not long before William returned, leading Frances, who very reluctantly yielded to accompany him.

"Come here," said her mamma, stopping the accusations she saw were ready to overwhelm the offending little girl; "come here, and let me talk to you about this sad thing you have done to the little birds. Do you see what you have done by your ill-judged kindness?"

"Kindness! mamma," they all exclaimed.

"Yes, dear children, she has been very faulty, but I believe she meant to be kind, and through ignorance did this thing which proves the death of the birds. *You* would not have done it, William, because you have already learnt there is such a thing as a necessary prudence to deal out your morsels with wisdom, and in a measure suited to the age and the capacity of the birds, and also that their food should be of a wholesome kind suitable to their nature. Nothing of this did Frances know, and it seems she had not learnt wisdom from the circumstances she had herself so lately fallen into.

"It reminds me of the scripture, which teaches us to profit: 'Open thy mouth wide, and I will fill it.' These little birds first attracted your attention by their *open mouths*, which they had stretched to receive what their poor mother was preparing to put into them. As one lighted on the edge of their nest, they instinctively opened their little yellow-edged beaks; she delighted to see them do so; and they, taking with content what she had provided for them, with the utmost confidence swallowed it down. She had a bit for every one of them in turn and they waited patiently until it was given them. All was well whilst they were nourished with parental tenderness and prudence, and none other meddled with them, or ventured to give them other things, which they, being blind, received and knew not the hand that gave, nor the consequences of eating food not such as their parent would have provided.

"Here you see Frances, neither prudent nor aware of consequences, has stuffed these little birds with improper food, both in quality and quantity. The consequences are fatal; one is dead, another is dying, and it is very uncertain whether the others also will not die. She fed them without measure, and their crops and throats were gorged so as to stop their breathing. They took it greedily, because they knew not the fatal consequences.

"Frances, you are a greedy girl. You had been suffering for this offence, and had not the wisdom to leave it to me to apportion your food. You opened your mouth wide, but you must remember it is not written that *you* are to fill it according to your own desires. 'I will fill it,' saith the Lord. He knows what is good for us, and he will measure his bounty according to his own wisdom."

Frances began to look ashamed and sorrowful.

"I was to you," her mamma continued, "in the affair of the cake, endeavoring to fulfil this my duty, but you rebelled against my discretion, and would covet more than was right. You ***helped yourself***, you gorged your stomach. You were cross and peevish, and ill, and when the medicine had relieved you, as it was designed, you, without reflection, sallied forth and suffocated the little birds. You could not feed them as the ***mother*** would. You could not find in the air and on the ground the little insects, and small worms and little grains which were their proper food, and you should have left it to their own mother to fill their opened mouths. ***She*** would have made no mistake either in the quality or quantity ***convenient*** for them."

"O," Mary said, "how that reminds me of the scripture in Proverbs xxx. 8: 'Feed me with food ***convenient*** for me.'"

"Yes, my dear girl, it's a scripture of great importance and often does it impress my mind in combination with the other I mentioned, Ps. lxxxi. 10: 'Open thy mouth wide, and *I* will fill it,' in their spiritual application, when I am providing for you, and dividing out your portions, and considering what diet is most suited to your constitution, and limiting the quantity of dainty or rich luxuries not *convenient* for you. I am also frequently led to apply it to myself, and to offer my petition to the Lord that he will graciously judge for me, both temporally and spiritually to *fill* my mouth, and feed me with food *convenient* for me."

"I think too, mamma, that there is some meaning belonging to this in our Lord's teaching us to pray, 'Give us this day our daily bread,' Matt. vi. 11."

"Assuredly, my dear child, and I am rejoiced to find you are led by this subject to compare spiritual things with spiritual.

"You see how the word of God interprets itself, and we are taught to go direct to the bounteous hand who giveth liberally, but never wastefully Our daily bread is sufficient for the day, and we must wait on him still for the daily bread of the succeeding day; so we are instructed to open our mouths wide to ask the Lord to fulfil his promise and to fill them, and to be contented with convenient food."

"O Mamma, you cannot think how many scriptures seem to come to my mind, and to give me a clearer understanding. You know the manna which was given in the wilderness, was *convenient* food when it was gathered daily as the Lord commanded, but when they laid it up, you know it was no longer *convenient,* for it stunk and bred worms. Does not this teach us to trust God as well as not to *disobey* him?"

"May this ready application of the word of God proceedeth from that grace, my child, which teaches you, like Job, to esteem the word of God more than your necessary food, for you will also remember what our Lord said to the tempter, 'It is written, Man does not live by *bread alone,* but *by every word* that proceeded out of the mouth of God.' But we are too apt to forget this, and to imagine that we can provide well for ourselves by fulfilling the desires and lusts of the flesh, and by so doing, we are likely to be brought to *forget* God, the bountiful and wise Supplier of all our wants."

"I remember the text, mamma, which has in it, 'Feed me with food *convenient* for me; and in another part, 'lest I be full and deny thee,' Prov. xxx. 9; and this little bird's nest has helped me to understand it better."

"May the Holy Spirit engrave it on your heart, for it will often remind you of the thankful contentedness with which you ought to wait on the Lord."

"Yes, mamma," William said, "but there is no harm, you know, in opening the mouth *wide*."

"No, William, certainly no *harm*, for it is a *duty*. 'Open thy mouth wide,' is an injunction of God, but it is immediately subjoined and strictly said, 'and I will fill it.' Therefore bear in mind the double instruction. Neither take the filling on yourself, nor be ready to swallow every crude and unwholesome morsel which the ignorant or the wicked would present to you. Do you remember a certain day last week when something happened?"

William looked anxious to recollect what his mamma alluded to, and in less than a minute he shook his head, and said, "Ah, mamma, that is too bad, you mean when Mrs. Arnot called, and you were out."

"Yes I do, William; you all opened your mouths wide, and *she* filled them. Her sweet things did not prove *convenient* food. You see, therefore, we should learn to discriminate between a heavenly Father's provision, and that of a stranger, whose busy interference may cost you your life. I was not many minutes away from my little nest, when a stranger came, and, by mistaken kindness made you all ill.

"Frances, have you never read that scripture: 'Put a knife to thy throat, if thou be a man given to appetite.'"

Frances cried, and, sobbing, said, "I do not know what it means?"

"What can it mean, my dear Frances, but parallel with those, 'If thy right eye offend thee, pluck it out if thy right hand offend thee, cut it off. It is better for thee to enter into life halt or maimed, than, having two hands or two feet, to be cast into everlasting fire,' Matt. xvvi. 29, 30. ii. 8, 9. It means that spirit which will sacrifice the lust of the heart, and deny itself, though it should be a present mortification. The *throat* of an inordinate or diseased appetite is to be cut, and its carnal desires crucified."

"Was it not something of this kind that Isaac fell into when he sent Esau to hunt venison, and make him savory meat, such as his soul loved? Gen. xxvii. 4."

"Yes, William, and this very thing he desired presented the temptation by which he was deceived. And you might have mentioned, too, how Esau himself yielded to his appetite, and sold his birthright for a mess of pottage, Gen. xxv. 29. When we yield to these propensities of the flesh, we lay a snare for our own souls, and expose our weakness to an adversary, ever ready to take advantage of our infirmity. It is a common fault in children to desire with greedy appetite such food as is pernicious, and to wish for more than even a mouth opened wide requires--till at length they learn to lust after *forbidden* things. And what does it lead to? Frances, you began to pick and steal, and your own iniquity chastised you:--you were sick and ill."

Frances hid her face in her frock.

"Ah mamma," said Anne, "I shall be afraid of wanting anything, as I used to do; and I hope I shall remember how much better you can feed me, than I can feed myself."

"I wish I may too," said William. "If Eve had but waited for the Lord only to fill her mouth, she would not have eaten that which brought sin and death."

"Tell me, Frances, if you feel the force of all we have learnt from the little birds, and your own mistaken idea of what would be good for them?"

Frances did not answer.

"But you know, my child, you were guilty of another fault; when the medicine was offered, which was likely to do you good,--you *refused* to open your mouth, and was long before you would let me fill it, so you see we must leave it all to the Lord to give us much or little, bitter or sweet, just as he knows to be *convenient* for us."

"Yes," Mary said, "these poor little birds will long teach us a lesson. We may imitate them to open our mouth wide, but we must be warned by what happened to them, to let the *Lord* only fill them."

"Let us look again at the nest." They approached, and frightened the mother so, that she flew off.

"See, see! William," said Anne, "the two little things are opening their mouths again. O how beautiful! let us never meddle with them any more. Only remember, 'Open thy mouth wide, and I will fill it.' Now, Frances, do not cry any more: come, we will bury these little dead birds."

Frances wiped her eyes, and Anne giving her a kiss, they went away to do as she proposed. After they had made a little coffin, they put the two little dead birds into it Then William got a spade, and dug a grave just large enough to hold the little coffin: and, as he lowered it into the grave, Mary wiped away the tears which gathered in her eyes. When William had filled up the grave, they all returned to their mamma, who said--

"My dear children, do not let us dismiss this interesting subject without a closer application. My dear Frances, come near to me, and hear what I have to say."

Frances drew near with some timidity. Conscious of her faults, and expecting the word of truth to be directed to her heart, she had at that moment rather have escaped from it. But her mamma, taking her hands into hers, and sitting down on a garden stool that was nigh, she felt that the words would be words of love, aid her heart beginning to soften, the tears were ready to flow, for she knew that her mamma would speak to her of Jesus and of his blood, which was shed for sinners.

"Do you know quite well, my child, that among the fruits of the Spirit enumerated, Gal. v., there is one called TEMPERANCE?"

"Yes, mamma," she replied.

"Are you not also conscious, my dear child, that your desire of indulging your appetite is quite contrary to this holy fruit?"

"Yes, mamma."

"Then what are you to do in order to overcome the one, and to obtain the other?"

"I must ask the Lord Jesus to give me the Holy Spirit."

"Yes, my child, to him must you come for all help, and he will not send you empty away. Here is a subject on which you must indeed open your mouth wide, in earnest prayer, and wait on the Lord for his gracious answer. 'Ask, and ye shall receive,' he says, and after showing how an *earthly* father will act towards his child that asks for bread, how does he conclude?"

"He says, 'How much *more* will your *heavenly* Father give the *Holy Spirit* to them that ask Him!'"

"Will you then, my dear Frances, profit by this gracious instruction, and will *you* ask for the Holy Spirit?"

"Yes, mamma, I will try."

"Do you believe the Lord will give you the Holy Spirit when you ask?"

"He *says* He *will*, mamma."

"That is enough, my child; what the Lord says is yea and amen. It is written, 'Hath he said, and will he not do it?'"

"Yes, mamma, I know God is *Truth*, He cannot lie."

"But you know also, my dear Frances, when the Holy Spirit is given, he takes up his abode in the heart, and he *acts* in the soul, and will not dwell there without producing his holy fruit; and tell me now what is the fruit you particularly want to overcome this sinful desire of appetite which prevails in your heart."

"Is it not *temperance*, mamma?"

"Yes, and if He comes into your heart, he will give it you, and moreover teach you to *repent* of your sins; for consider, my Frances, sin is an offence against him, and needs to be repented of. Do you repent?"

"I am very sorry, mamma."

"But repentance is more than sorrow; it will make you ashamed before God, and make you feel yourself vile; and it will also make you carefully watchful against the temptation; it will make you anxious to quit the sin, and clear your soul from its power; it will make you indignant against it, and urge you to seek that strength from the Spirit, which will resist the sin, and overcome it. When, therefore, you ask for the Holy Spirit, be *willing* that the Lord should *fill* you. Be ready to *exercise* the mighty gift for *all* his offices, to convict you of sin, to lead you to true expectations, and to strengthen you to overcome your sin, giving you that grace which is specially opposed to the leading sin of your heart."

"I wish I had this gift; for my sin makes me very unhappy: I know it is wrong."

"Do not stop in *wishes*, dear child, go and *pray*; 'Ask, and ye shall receive.' 'Open your mouth wide' in the full utterance of all your distress, and of all you desire; pray for what you *want, name* it; pray for *repentance*, and for *temperance*. Pray that the *lust of your appetite* may be *crucified*, and pray that the blood of Jesus, the Lamb of God who taketh away sin, may be sprinkled upon your guilty soul, and cleanse it from all sin. He giveth liberally, and upbraideth not. He is angry only when we neglect his promises and his gifts.

"It is not long since, dear Mary, that you and I conversed on this text, 'My people would not hearken to my voice, Israel would none of me: *so I gave them up to their own heart's lusts*,' Psa. lxxxi. A dreadful judgment! what would become of *you*, dear Frances, if you were given up to the dominion of your appetite?"

"But, my dear mamma," Mary said, "do you not remember the end of that psalm, what a sweet verse there is?"

"Repeat it, dear girl, and let little Frances hear it!"

"'*Had* they hearkened and obeyed, then should he have fed them with the finest of the wheat, and with honey out of the rock should I have satisfied them.'"

"O my children," said their mamma, "here is spiritual food for the spiritual appetite! You know who is the Bread of Life, and who is the Rock of our salvation. Turn unto him your whole heart, and though you feel the burden of the body of this death, you shall soon be able to thank God, who, through Jesus Christ our Lord, will deliver you."

"Poor Esau repented too late,
That once he his birth-right despis'd,
And sold for a morsel of meat,
What could not too highly be priz'd.
How great was his anguish when told,
The blessing he sought to obtain
Was gone with the birth-right he sold,
And none could recall it again!
  He stands as a warning to all,
Wherever the gospel shall come!
O hasten and yield to the call,
While yet for repentance there's room!
Your season will quickly be past;
Then hear and obey it to-day,
Lest when you seek mercy at last,
The Saviour should frown you away.

What is it the world can propose?
A morsel of meat at the best!
For this are you willing to lose
A share in the joys of the blest?
Its pleasures will speedily end,
Its favor and praise are but breath;
And what can its profits befriend

Your soul in the moments of death?

If Jesus, for these, you despise,
And sin to the Saviour prefer,
In vain your entreaties and cries,
When summon'd to stand at his bar:
How will you his presence abide?
What anguish will torture your heart,
The saints all enthron'd by his side,
And you be compelled to depart.

Too often, dear Saviour, have I
Preferr'd some poor trifle to thee;
How is it thou dost not deny
The blessing and birth-right to me?
No better than Esau I am,
Though pardon and heaven be mine
To me belongs nothing but shame,
The praise and the glory be thine."

I.
The Little Pavior.

"Even a child is known by his doings, whether his work be pure, and whether it be right,"--PROVERBS, xx. 11.

Happy the child who is active, intelligent and obliging, and who takes pleasure in serving those that are about him! Happy above all is the child, who, fearing and loving the Lord, shows himself thus zealous and obliging, from a feeling of piety, and a desire to please God.

Such was Francis, and this we shall soon see, from the following narrative:

Francis, who was about eight years old, was spending the month of June with his Grandpapa in the country.

His Grandpapa lived in a pretty house, roofed with slates, and surrounded with a verandah, in which were seats, and between each seat, some flower-pots. Jessamine and roses entwined themselves around the verandah, and adorned it with elegant festoons of flowers.

Behind the house was a yard, where chickens, turkeys, and guinea- fowls, were kept; and in the front, looking towards the west, was laid out a fine garden, well provided with evergreens, such as holly, yew, and pine-trees, and amongst these, also, many birch and ash- trees flourished.

At the bottom of the garden, which sloped a little, flowed a pure, but shallow stream, which was crossed by means of a wooden bridge, surrounded with elders and large hazels.

This was a delightful dwelling-place, but those who inhabited it, were still more delightful than the beautiful garden or the smiling groves. For it was the beauty of piety which was found in them, united with that gentleness and amiability of character, that humble spirit of cordiality, which our Saviour enjoins upon all his true disciples.

These inhabitants, so good and so amiable, were the Grandpapa and Grandmamma of Francis, and their domestics, who, with them served the Lord, and lived in that peace, which His Spirit gives to such as delight in His Word.

This dear Grandpapa then, since he was pious, was charitable, and took particular pleasure in visiting his aged neighbors, especially the poor peasants, to whom he always carried comfort and encouragement from that gracious God, with whom he himself daily endeavored more and more to live. He used generally to pay these charitable visits in the middle of the day; after having read the Holy Bible for the second time, in a retired summer-house in the garden, near which a little gate opened upon a footpath, which, passing through the orchard, led to the village.

Francis, who was already acquainted with his Grandpapa's habits, never came to disturb him while he was in the summer-house, and whenever he saw his Grandpapa going out of the little gate he took good care not to follow him.

But in about an hour or two, he would go to meet him, sometimes towards the road, at others, as far as the bridge over the stream;-- his Grandmamma was never uneasy, because she knew that Francis was a prudent boy, and that God watched over him, as one of the lambs of the good shepherd.

Grandpapa then, had just finished reading; he had put on his hat and taken his cane, and had gone out through the gate.

Francis, who was sitting before the house, under the pretty green verandah, saw him pass behind the garden hedge, and was already thinking of going to meet him at the end of an hour, when to his great surprise he saw his Grandpapa pass again behind the hedge, and then enter the garden through the little gate, walking apparently with much difficulty.

"What is the matter, dear Grandpapa?" cried Francis, springing towards the garden.--"Oh! how you are covered with mud! It must be that rude Driver who wanted to fawn upon you. He has always such dirty paws."

"You must not scold Driver, but *me*," mildly replied his Grandpapa, "for I incautiously, and most imprudently, walked upon that part of the path which has been inundated by the water from the fountain."

"Grandpapa, did you fall?" asked Francis, quite alarmed.

"Yes my boy, your Grandfather fell like a heedless man.... But thanks to our gracious God, who ever takes care of us! it was nothing; I was only a little frightened. You see, Francis, you must not forget that we only stand, because God supports us."

So saying, his Grandfather entered the house, and with the same serenity related his accident to his wife, who bestowed every attention upon him.

Whilst his Grandfather was resting himself, and Francis had ascertained that he had not suffered much, he hastened to look at the spot where his kind Grandpapa had slipped and fallen. It was a little bit of the path, perhaps about three paces long, covered with the water which was issuing from the fountain, and which being of clay, had become very slippery.

The trench round the fountain had been already deepened more than once, in order to turn its course from that part of the orchard, but as the ground was rather low, the water always returned.

Francis examined all this, and tried to find out what could be done to remedy the evil, in a more durable manner.

"*I know!*" he cried at last. "I must make a pavement here, a little higher than the path is at present!"

"Come! cheer up! 'Where there's a will,' says Grandpapa, 'with God's help there's a way.' To work, to work! 'For he who does nothing makes little progress,' says also, my dear Grandpapa."

It may be here well asked, how a little child, eight years of age, could even conceive such a project, and much more how he could have had sufficient strength to accomplish it.

But Francis was not a thoughtless or inattentive child; on the contrary he observed on his way *to*, and *from* School, and when he walked out with his Papa, everything that workmen did.

It was thus that he had often noticed how the Paviors first laid down the stones, and then pressed them together, and as we shall soon see, he found no difficulty in what he was going to attempt.

"First and foremost," said he, "the tools!" and immediately he ran off to look for a little wheel-barrow which his Grandpapa had made for him; with the spade, the trowel, and the iron rake, which were at his disposal.

When the tools were collected, Francis, having taken off his jacket, traced out the portion to be paved.

"Now," said he, "I must take away two or three inches of earth, that the stones may fit in."

He then took away the earth, and piled it up on the upper side of the path, in order to compel the water to pass by the drain.

"Now," he said, "I must find some sand; where is there any? Oh! behind the hen-house; the masons, who plastered the walls of the yard over again, have left a large heap of it there"--and then he quickly ran with his wheelbarrow, once, twice, and even three times, and soon had as much as was necessary. He spread it out, and arranged it, and then pronounced the great word of all his work, "*Stones!* No stones, no pavement! I must have at least fifty of them!" He ran about, searched and gathered, near the fountain, round the house, and along the wall of the yard, and soon brought back four wheelbarrows full of nice stones, well shaped, and not too large.

But there were not enough, for he was obliged to put five or six abreast. Where are there any more to be found?

"In the brook," cried he! "It is rather far off, but I shall soon be there!" And indeed in about a quarter of an hour, he had collected all the proper materials.

Then should he have been seen at work! The trowel in his right hand, a stone in his left; the sand which he placed between each stone, and the blows which forced it down, these things succeeded each other rapidly, and were often repeated; till at length, at the end of the third hour, the slippery bit of foot-path was no longer in existence, but in its stead was to be seen a pavement slightly raised, which could never be wetted by the overflowing of the fountain.

"That will not do well," said Francis, when he had finished, and was walking over the pavement; "it is uneven, Grandpapa will hurt his feet upon it." And so saying, he ran to the woodhouse in the yard, and returned, bending under the weight of the mallet, with which Thomas used to strike the axe and wedges, when he split the large pieces of oak.

"Here is *my* rammer," said Francis, laughing, as he thought of those used by the paviors; and holding the mallet perpendicularly, he struck with the butt-end, first one stone, and then another, until at length the pavement was completed! It was solid, even and clean, and Francis, repeating in truth, "Where there's a will, with God's help, there's a way," gave thanks in his heart to that good heavenly Father, who gave him both the idea and the will to do this act of filial love, and enabled him to accomplish it.

Some sand and a few stones remained; Francis took them up and carried them back near to the house. Then he cleared away the rubbish, and having put on his coat again, returned joyfully to replace his tools in the green-house.

All this was done after dinner, between the hours of three and six. The evening passed quietly away. Grandpapa had not received any bruises, and he could not sufficiently thank the Good shepherd, the Lord Jesus, who had, as it were, "carried him in his arms," and "kept all his bones."

Grandmamma joined in his praises and thanksgivings, and these two faithful servants blessed the Lord together, whose mercies are over all his works.

"To-morrow, please God," said Grandpapa to Francis, "I shall go and see old George. He must have expected me to-day! But be assured, my dear Francis, that your Grandpapa will walk no more like a giddy child; and if the path is still slippery, I shall place my foot prudently upon it."

Francis said he hoped the path would be better; and however that might be, that the Lord would preserve him thenceforth from slipping, and above all, from falling.

Grandpapa made Francis read the Bible as usual to the whole household. He spoke piously of God's paternal care for our bodies as well as for our souls, and in his prayer he gave abundant thanks to the Saviour who had so graciously preserved him.

The morrow came. Grandpapa had quite recovered his accident of the preceding day, and after reading in the summer-house, he got up to go and see old George.

Francis, who was observing him from beneath the verandah, no sooner saw him come near the little gate, than he ran round the house to hide himself behind a hazel bush, a short distance from the pavement, in order to see what his Grandpapa would do.

Grandpapa walked on towards the orchard, and as soon as he set his foot on the path, he prepared to proceed very carefully. He took three or four steps, and then suddenly stopped, and raising his hands, exclaimed, a "pavement! a pavement here already! How does this happen? Who could have done this? It must be my faithful Thomas!"--he continued--"I must thank him for it;" and he called out loudly, "Thomas! Thomas!" Thomas, who was in the cow-house, heard his voice, and ran to him in alarm.

"Have you tumbled again, sir," he asked anxiously?

"On the contrary," said Grandpapa, "thanks to *you*, Thomas, for having made this good substantial pavement so quickly and so well; it is really excellent," said he, stamping upon it with his foot, and walking over it in every direction. "It is solid, and even, and slopes on either side! I am very much obliged to you, Thomas."

"Alas! sir," said the man, "it is not I who did it--how vexed I am that I did not think of it what stupidity!"...

"Who is it then?" asked Grandpapa, "for this has been done since yesterday, and surely these stones are not mushrooms! Who could have thought of this?"

"I think I know who it is, sir," answered Thomas, "for yesterday in the afternoon I saw master Francis going down to the brook with his wheelbarrow. I could not think what it was for, but now I understand."

"Francis! did you say," exclaimed Grandpapa; "how could that child have done it even if he had wished? Are these stones only nuts, that *that* dear boy's little hands could have been able to knock them into the ground?"

"Do you wish, sir, that I should look for him and bring him here?" asked Thomas.

Francis could no longer remain concealed. He ran from behind the bush, and threw himself into his Grandpapa's arms; saying, "Dear Grandpapa, how happy I am to have been able to succeed."

"It is *you* then, indeed, my son!" cried Grandpapa, as he shed tears of joy. "God bless your filial piety towards me! May He return you two-fold all the good you have done my heart. But how did you manage?"

"You have often told me, dear Grandpapa, that 'Where there's a will, with the help of God, there's a way,' and I prayed to God, and was able to do it."

"Well then, dear Francis," said Grandpapa, solemnly, "I promise you, that every day of my life, as long as I shall walk here below, when I pass over this pavement, which your affection has made for me, I will say to God 'O Lord, prevent Francis from falling in his way! May thy goodness *pave* for him the path of life, whenever it becomes slippery.'"

Francis understood, and respectfully received this blessing; and whilst his Grand father paid his visit, the little pavior went and told his Grandmamma, what he had been able to do, and how God had already blessed him for it.

II.
The Silver Knife.

"Then said Jesus unto him: Go and do thou likewise."--LUKE, x. 37.

Mary.--(After having searched about the dining-room,) "Who has seen my silver knife? William, John, Lucy, you who are amusing yourselves in the garden, have you seen my silver knife?"

William.--(Going up to the window, and in a sententious tone of voice,) "'Disorder,' says an ancient writer, 'occasions sorrow, and negligence, blame.'"

Mary.--"Admirable! But that does not apply to *me*, for it is scarcely an hour since I laid my knife on this very table, which certainly belongs to us."

Lucy.--"Are you quite sure of it, Mary!"

Mary--"Yes, indeed, there is no doubt of it, for Sophy asked me to give her a pretty little red apple, as usual, before going to school. I went immediately to the fruit-room for it, and as it was a little spoiled, I cleaned it with my silver knife, which I laid on this table, whilst I was kissing her. I am therefore quite sure of it."

John.--(Frowning,)--"For my part, I confess, I don't like all these strangers who come about the house. For instance, that little *Jane*, who sells lilies of the valley, and strawberries, and so on--I very much distrust her sullen look; and who knows, if perhaps...?"

Lucy--"Fie, fie, brother, to suspect that poor little modest gentle child, who supports her sick mother by her own industry! Oh! it is very wrong, John!"

"What is the matter?" said their Father, who had heard this dispute from the garden, where he was reading under the shade of a tree.

Mary related her story, and finished by saying,--"Well, if it be God's will, So-be-it! My beautiful knife is lost!"

"Yes, my dear girl," answered her father, "What God wills, is always best. But it is His will that I should watch over, my household. I must therefore know what has become of your knife. Did you ask Elizabeth if she had taken care of it, when she cleaned the room?"

Mary ran to the kitchen, and enquired of Elizabeth.

"Your silver knife! Miss," said the servant, coloring. "Have you lost that beautiful knife, which was given you on your birthday?"

"I ask you, if you have taken care of it," answered Mary. "I laid it this morning upon the table in the dining-room, near the window."

Elizabeth.--(with astonishment,)--Near the window! Oh!--I know where it is, now. About half an hour ago, when I went into the dining-room, to ... put ... down ... some plates, I saw the great magpie, which builds its nest up in the large elm-tree, at the end of the garden, sitting on the window-ledge. It flew away as soon as it saw me; but it had something white and shining in its beak. Oh! yes, I remember now! it was the silver knife!"

"The magpie," exclaimed Mary, "with my knife in its beak!"

"Oh! Miss," replied Elizabeth, "there is no thief like a magpie. When I was at home, one of their nests was once pulled down, and nine pieces of silver were found in it, and a whole necklace of pearls! Oh! magpies are terrible birds, and you may be sure that your knife is in their nest."

Mary returned to her father in the garden, and related to him all that Elizabeth had said, but added, "For my part, I don't believe a word of it!"

"And why not?" exclaimed John, sharply, "Elizabeth is quite right! Nothing steals like a magpie. Everybody says so. Come! let us to work! A ladder, a cord, and a long stick! Down with the nest!--Papa, will you allow me to climb the tree!"

Lucy.--(Holding John by the arm.)--"Brother, how *can* you think of it? The elm is more than eighty feet high! Papa, I beg of you, not to allow it."

Father.--(Calmly.)--"No one shall get up the tree and risk his life, for a thing which certainly is not there."

"There is no thief like a magpie," repeated John, looking at the nest, which might be seen through the higher branches of the tree; "but I confess it would not be easy to reach it. These branches are very long and very slender!"

William, who had said nothing as yet, but had been walking backwards and forwards, with his head down, and his hands in his pockets, turned suddenly round to Mary, and said, "I have been thinking we can soon know if your knife is in the nest. We only want a polemoscope for that. Hurrah! long live optics!"

"A lemoscope!" said Lucy, "What is that? Is it a long hook?"

William.--(Smiling rather contemptuously.) "Poor sister! What ignorance!"

Father--"William, speak kindly--tell your sister what this instrument is, and what you want to do with it."

William.--(Scientifically.)--"In war, when a besieged garrison wishes to know all the movements of the enemy, without being seen, they erect behind the walls, or the ramparts, a mirror, placed at the end of a long pole, and inclining towards the country. You understand, then, that everything that takes place outside, is reflected in the mirror, and can be seen from within, or in another mirror placed at the bottom of the pole, and sloping inwards. This, Lucy, is what is called a polemoscope-- that is to say, an instrument for observations in war."

"Thank you, William," said Lucy, "but what are you going to do with it?"

William.--"The thing is quite plain. I am going to fasten a small mirror on a light pitchfork, inclining it downwards. This pitchfork I shall fasten firmly to pole; then some one will climb, dear papa, without any danger, as far as the strong branches reach; from thence he can draw up the pole and its mirror, with a long string, and by raising the mirror above the nest, he will enable us to see, with the aid of your telescope, all that the nest contains. This is my plan, and I think it is not so bad!"

Father.--(Smiling.)--"Dear William. It is a great pity, however, that you are so blind. There are two things you have not considered. One is, that the branches which cover the nest, are very thick and tufted. Therefore, your mirror, even if it reached their summit, would only reflect the leaves, and consequently neither the nest nor the knife; and the other thing which you do not observe, is this, that the magpies, by an admirable instinct, which God has given them, build their nests, not like a basin, as you supposed, but in the form of a ball; so that the nest is covered with a vaulted roof, formed of sticks closely interwoven, which shelters the bird and its brood from bad weather, and above all, from the cruel claw of the kite or hawk."

"I am much obliged to you, dear papa," said William. "What a pity," he added, with a sigh; "for my plan would otherwise have been infallible."

"Let us seek a better one," said their father. "Mary, go and see if you have not left your knife in the fruit-room. Perhaps it was yesterday, that you peeled the apple for Sophy."

"I will do so," said Mary, and she went into the house for the key of the fruit-room.

She soon returned, exclaiming, "The key is not in its place, and I put it there this morning."

"Miss Mary is mistaken," said Elizabeth, coming out of the kitchen; "I see the key in the door."

"Papa," said Mary, "I recollect, when I put the key in the cupboard, this very morning, Sophy looked at it, and said, 'It is certainly the prettiest key on the bunch.'"

"Let us go to the fruit-room," said the father, directing his steps thither. "I fear this will prove a sad affair."

"What is this, too," cried Mary, examining the shelves, "the big key of the cellar here Where did it come from? And this key covered with cheese, from one end to the other!"

"Let us go to the cellar!" said the father. "I believe we shall find out more there than we can here."

They opened the door, and found the brilliant silver knife, not in the magpie's nest, but sticking in a cheese, from which a large portion appeared to have been detached.

The children were amazed, and their Father much grieved.

"Here is your knife, Mary," said John, who first saw it. "Certainly, there is no need of a looking-glass to find it."

"You must not joke, my children," said the Father; "this is a very sad business. I am thankful it has taken place in the absence of your dear Mother, and I forbid you writing her anything about it. This must concern me, and me alone."

William.--(Indignantly.)--"It amounts to a theft, a falsehood!"

Lucy.--"But who has done it, William? Did not Mary leave her knife here?"

William.--"Who saw the Magpie carrying it off in his beak?"

Mary.--(To Lucy.)--"Do you not understand that it was poor Elizabeth, who came here with my knife, which she took off the table where I left it, and who, after having cut a piece of cheese with it, went to the fruit-room, no doubt to steal some apples also."

John.--(Angrily.)--"Papa, Elizabeth has acted deceitfully-- will you allow her to remain with you? One of the Psalms, the 101st, I think, says, 'He that worketh deceit shall not dwell within my house.'"

The Father.--(Gravely.) "It is said also in Holy Scriptures, my son, that 'mercy rejoiceth against judgment,' and perhaps, John, if any of us, had been brought up like poor Elizabeth, we might have done even worse than this."

"I am quite vexed," said Mary, "Oh! why did I not take more care of that wretched knife!"

William.--"But, Mary, it was not your knife left upon the table, which tempted her to take two keys secretly out of the cupboard, and which made them the instruments of this theft. For Papa," continued he, "it *is* a theft, and a shameful one too! These stolen keys are no small matter!"

The Father.--(Calmly.)--"I know it my children, and it grieves my heart, that one of my servants, who daily hears the word of God read and explained, should so far have forgotten the fear of the Lord! This is what saddens me, and wounds me deeply."

Lucy.--"Elizabeth has not long been our cook, and probably she never heard the word of God before she came here. Poor girl I she is perhaps very unhappy now,--and I am sure, she will repent and turn to God."

The Father.-"That is right, my dear child, I rejoice to hear you plead the cause of the unhappy, and even of the guilty, for as I said before, 'mercy rejoiceth against judgment.'"

"I was therefore wrong," said John, "and I confess it ... for certainly I scarcely pitied her.... I did wrong I and now I think as Lucy does."

"And I also," said William, "'Clemency governs courage,' says a Grecian historian, and ..."

The Father.--(Very seriously.)--"But, my dear William, what have the pagans of old and their morals to do here? My son, you know it is the word of God which rules our conduct, and which commands us to suffer and to forgive."

Lucy.--"Papa, will you allow me to repeat a passage, which I learnt by heart last Sunday?"

The Father.--"Repeat it, Lucy, and may God bless it to us all!"

Lucy.--"'Execute true judgment, and show mercy and compassion every man to his brother.' It is in the seventh chapter of Zechariah."

"I too, was wrong then," said William, "very wrong! for it is the wisdom of God alone, that enlightens us."

"True, my son," said his Father, "may God always remind you of this. I am going to speak to Elizabeth," he added, "as for you, my children, do not say a word about it, and above all, bless the Lord, for having made known to you his grace and holy law. Pray to him together, that my words may have their due effect upon the mind of this poor guilty creature."

The Father went out to look for Elizabeth, and the children repaired to William's room, who, having knelt down with them, prayed to the Lord to take pity upon her, and to touch her heart, and he ended the prayer in the following words:--"In thy great wisdom, O Most Gracious God, and in thine infinite compassion, through Jesus Christ, grant unto each of us true repentance, and a sincere change of heart, and may this affliction be turned to the glory of our Saviour Jesus."

The children then returned to their several occupations, and not one of them ever thought of judging Elizabeth, or even speaking harshly of her.

We may add, that the exhortation of her charitable master, produced sincere penitence in Elizabeth, and that the poor girl was not sent out of the house; for "mercy pleaded against judgment."

It is thus that God deals with us! Oh! which of us can tell how often he has received pardon from the Lord!

III.
The Modern Dorcas

"The night cometh when no man can work."--JOHN, ix.

Oh! my sister! my sister! What a lesson may we learn from the death of our dear Amelia! She was but sixteen years old like myself, and only two years older than you are, but how much had she done for the Lord. I saw and heard her, when Jesus came to call her to himself; I was in the churchyard when they placed her body in the grave! Oh! what a solemn warning! and now I feel humbled before God, and I pray Him to pour into my heart the same Spirit which He bestowed so abundantly upon our friend, as well as that lively faith, which although Amelia 'is dead, yet speaketh,' as it is said of Abel, and which shall speak through her for many years to come!

I wrote to you less than a fortnight ago, that Amelia was unwell; but how little I then thought it was her last illness! Oh! how uncertain our life is, dear Esther, and how much wiser we should be if we would only believe so!

On the seventh day of her illness, her mother said to me, "Anna, your friend is going to leave us; the danger of her disorder increases every hour, and we must give her up to God!"

I wept much and bitterly, and could not at first believe it; but when I was alone with Amelia, the next day, she said to me, with that calm peacefulness which never left her, "I am going away from this world, Anna; yes, dear Anna, I am going to depart; I feel it, and ... I am preparing myself for it!"

I tried to turn away her thoughts from this subject; I told her that she was mistaken, and that God would certainly restore her; but she stopped me with firmness of manner, and said, "Do you envy my happiness, Anna? Do you wish to prevent me from going to my Heavenly home, to my Saviour, unto his light and glory?" The entrance of her father and the Doctor prevented my reply, and I left the room in tears.

"You must not cry," said her mother to me. "We must pray, and above all, seek profit from the occasion. The time is short! Her end is at hand! But," added this servant of Christ, "*that* end is the beginning of a life which shall have no end!"

Three more days passed away. On the fourth, we had some faint hope, but the following day, all had vanished, and towards evening, Amelia declared, that the Lord was about to take her.

"Yes, my dear parents, my excellent father and mother," she said, with a beam of heavenly joy on her countenance, "I am about to leave you; but I do not leave my God, for I am going to see Him, 'face to face.'"

"My dear parents," she continued, affectionately, "rejoice at my departure; I am going to Heaven a little before you, it is true, but it is *only before you*, and you know it; and the Apostle says, that, 'to be with Christ is far better.'"

I was present, Esther, and was crying.

"Why do you cry, Anna?" she said, "Are you sorry to see me go to my Father's house?"

"But, Amelia, *I* lose you; we all lose you; and ..."

"I do not like to hear you say that, Anna; do not repeat it, and do not think of it. Our Saviour says that, 'He who believes on Him shall not see death;' and I am certain, that my soul is about to join those of His saints who have already departed this life, for His grace has also justified *me.*"

"Ah!" said her aunt, who had not left her bedside for two days, "you have always done the will of God, dear Amelia; you are therefore sure of going to Him."

"Dear aunt," she replied, with sorrow on her countenance, "I assure you that you grieve me. I have been during the whole of my life, but a poor sinner, and have by no means done what you say; but.... God Himself has pardoned me, and it is only, my dear aunt, because the blood of Jesus has washed away my sins, that I shall see God."

It was thus, my sister, that Amelia spoke at intervals almost the whole night. Her voice at length became weaker; and towards morning, after a slight drowsiness, she said to her father, "Papa, embrace your child once more." She then turned to her mother, and said, "My dear mamma, embrace me also, and ... may Jesus comfort you all!"

A few minutes after, our darling friend fell gradually asleep, and her last breath died away like the expiring flame of a candle. She experienced nothing of the agony of death. Truly, dear Esther, Amelia knew not what death was!

But oh! how I have myself suffered! and how difficult it is to tear one's self thus forever here below, from such a friend as she was!

Nevertheless, my sister, God knows we have not dared to murmur. I wish you had heard the prayer that Amelia's father offered up, when his daughter had ceased to breathe! Oh! it was the spirit of consolation itself which spoke! And since that solemn hour, what piety, what strength and peace of mind, Amelia's mother his displayed! I am sure you would have said, that the Lord was present, and that He was telling us with His own voice: "Amelia triumphs--she is in *My* glory!"

I wished to be in the churchyard when our friend, or rather, when her body of dust, was committed to the grave. There were many persons present, but especially poor people; some old men, and several children, came to take their last leave of her.

A grey-headed and feeble old man was standing near the grave, leaning with his two hands on a staff, and with his head depressed. He wept aloud, when the clergyman mentioned Amelia's name, as he prayed, and gave thanks to God. He then stooped down, and taking a little earth in his hand, said, as he scattered it over the coffin: "Sleep, sweet messenger of consolation! Sleep, until He whom thy lips first proclaimed to me, calls thee to arise!" And with this, he burst into tears, as they filled the grave.

When all was finished, and the funeral procession had departed, the poor people who were present approached the grave, sobbing, and repeating, "Sweet messenger of goodness! Our kind friend, our *true* mother!" And two or three of the children placed upon her grave nosegays of box and white flowers.

"Alas," said a young girl, "she will never hear me read the Bible again, nor instruct me how to live!"

Another cried loudly, "Who will now come to visit my sick mother, and read the Bible to her, and bring her comfort and assistance."

And there was a father, a poor workman, with two little boys, who, holding his children by the hand, came and placed himself near the spot where the head of Amelia was laid, saying to them, "Here, my poor children, under this sod, rests that sweet countenance which used to smile upon you, as if she had been your mother! Her lips have often told you, that you were not orphans, and that God was better to you than a parent.... Well, my dear children, let us remember what she used to say: 'God has not forgotten us, and He will sustain us!'"

I was with my brother, who himself wept with all his heart, to see the sincere grief of these poor people. He whispered to me, "I have a great mind to speak to them, and ask them what Amelia used to do for them." I had the same wish; so we approached a group which surrounded the grave, and asked them when they had become acquainted with Amelia.

"For my part," answered the old man, already spoken of, "this messenger of peace visited me two years ago, for the first time. I lived near a family to whom she had brought some worsted stockings, for winter was just setting in, and so my neighbor mentioned me to her, as a poor infirm old man. She desired to see me, and had she been my own daughter, she could never have shown me more respect and kindness! She procured me a warm quilt that same evening, and on the morrow, towards the middle of the day, she came with her excellent mother to pay me a long visit.

"You must know, sir," continued the old man, to my brother, "I was then very ignorant, or rather my heart was hard and proud towards God. I had no Bible, and did not care about one. Well, this dear young lady not only brought me one, with her own hands, but came to read and explain it to me, with great patience, at least three times a week, during the first twelve months.

"God took pity on me," added the old man, in a low voice, "and last year I began better to understand the full pardon which is in Christ Jesus, and was even able to pray with Miss Amelia.

"She used sometimes to call me, 'My old father,' but it was I who ought to have called *her* the *mother*, the true mother of my soul.

"Just one month ago, she came to me for the last time; she gave me with a sweet smile, these worsted gloves, which she had knitted herself, and then recommended me with much respect and kindness to thank our Lord, who sent them me! This was the last of that sweet lady's charities to me!"...

Upon this, the old man turned away weeping, and as he walked slowly on, he frequently looked back upon the newly-covered grave.

"The same thing happened to me," said the workman. "The mother of these two little children died ten months ago; we were in want of everything, then, and I knew not even how to dress these children. Believe me, Miss," he added, addressing me with feeling, "when the mother is gone, all is gone!... but our gracious God did not forsake us, for He sent us his angel; I say His angel, although she is at present much more than an angel!... Is she not indeed a child of God in heaven? ... but, in short, she clothed these two little ones, and I am sure she did not spare herself in working for them; the clothes they now wear were made chiefly by that dear young lady's hands. Then she used to come and visit us; she often made my two children go to her house, and always gave them good advice. She also sent them to school, and although it was certainly her mother who paid for them, yet it was Miss Amelia who taught them to read at home, and who, almost every Sunday, made them repeat their Bible lessons.

"Ah, Miss," he continued, "all that that dear young lady did for us, for our souls as well as for our bodies, will only be known in heaven, and at the last day. For my part, and I say it here over her grave, and in the presence of God, I am certain, that when the Lord Jesus shall raise us all up again, the works of Miss Amelia will follow her, and we shall then see that while upon earth she served God with all her heart.

"No," he added, as he wiped away the tears from his children's eyes, "I would not wish her to return from the glory which she now enjoys, at the same time I cannot conceal from you, that my heart mourns for her, and that I know we have lost our consolation, our benefactress, our faithful friend!"

"Who has not lost one?" exclaimed a poor woman, at whose side stood the little girls who had planted the flowers; "I know very well that Miss Amelia's mother will take her place, she is so good and kind! but it was no little joy to receive a visit from that sweet and amiable young lady, so good, so pious, and so full of joy. Oh! what should I have done with my husband, so long confined to his bed, if this messenger of goodness had not procured work for me, and recommended me to the ladies who now employ me. And then again, what were we, until Miss Amelia spoke to us? How much she had to put up with when I refused to read the Holy Scriptures! and yet she was never weary of me. Oh! no; she came day after day, to exhort and to teach me, and blessed be God, we begin now to know something of what the Saviour has done for us.

"And," added she, drawing the little girl towards her, "I shall go on with my dear children, reading and learning that word of God, which was Miss Amelia's greatest joy.

"Come, come, my friends," she said, in a persuasive tone, "*we* must also die, and be put each in his turn, under this ground; but as our benefactress is not dead ... (no, she is not dead, for the Lord has said it!)--so also shall not we die, if we follow in her steps."

The poor woman then wished us good day, and moved away with her children. We all walked on together, still speaking of Amelia. My brother took the names and addresses of many of the poor people, with whom he had just been conversing, and spoke a few words to them of comfort and encouragement.

As soon as we were alone, he showed me the list of names, at the head of which was that of the old man, and he said, "Here is a blessed inheritance which Amelia has left us. She has done as Dorcas did: her hands have clothed the poor, and her lips have spoken comfort to them. Dear Anna, Amelia was not older than we are; let us remember this, for we know not when the Lord shall call us."

How wise and pious this dear brother is! We have already been able to pay together, two of Amelia's visits. Her mother, to whom we related all we had heard, gave us further particulars of what the pious and indefatigable Amelia used to do. Ah Esther, her religion was not mere "lip-service." The Spirit of the Lord Jesus Christ assisted her, and she might have said with truth, I show "my faith by my works."

Let us take courage, then, my dear and kind sister! we lament our loss in Amelia's death, but on her own account I lament her not. I can only contemplate her in the presence of God, and of her Saviour, and I rejoice to think of her delight when she entered the region of heaven. How beautiful it must be, Esther, to behold the glory of that heaven! to hear the voices of saints and angels, and to know that God loves us, and will make us happy forever.

Think, sister, of the meaning of--*forever!*

Amelia's father, whom I saw a few hours ago with her excellent and pious mother, said to me, in speaking of their darling child, "For my own joy and comfort I should have wished to have kept her with us; but, my dear Anna, even if I could have done so, what would have been all our happiness, compared with that which she now possesses in the presence of her God."

But do not suppose, my sister, that Amelia, with all her piety, was less prudent with regard to the things of this world, than faithful regarding those of heaven. Her mother has shown me her books, and her different arrangements, all of which indicate that discretion spoken of in Scripture, carried out in the most minute particulars.

First, as respects order and cleanliness in everything belonging to her: it would be impossible to imagine a more proper arrangement than the one she made of each article, both in her wardrobe, her writing- table, her work-box, and her account-book.

She had not much money to devote to her works of charity, but her industry made up for her limited means; for instance, in opening the Bible which she generally made use of, I found in it, four or five pages written with a great deal of care; and her journal informed her mother, who read it, of the reason of this circumstance. It runs thus:

"As old Margaret has but one Bible, some of the leaves of which have been lost, I have given her mine, which is quite complete, and have taken hers, adding to it some sheets of paper, upon which I have written the passages which were deficient. Thus I have saved the expense of a new Bible; and it is the same thing to me."

Amelia's diary is very remarkable; her mother has allowed me to read many portions of it, and to copy out what relates to her usual manner of employing each day. I send it to you, dear Esther, and you will find, as I have done, that the Spirit of God always teaches those who trust in Him, how precious *time* is here below. The following is what our dear friend wrote upon this subject.

"*January 1st*, 1844--Nearly eighteen centuries, and a half have passed away, since our Saviour took upon himself the form of human flesh for our salvation. Those years seemed long as they succeeded each other, but now that they are gone, they appear as nothing.

"Families, and nations, and the mighty generations of mankind, which, in times gone by, peopled the earth, have all passed away. Nothing remains of them here below!

"But such is not the case in heaven,--I should rather say,--in eternity. There, all these nations still exist, no man can be absent, but must appear before the Sovereign Judge, to answer for the use which he has made of his time.

"How short that time is! Where are the years that David lived, and where are those which Methuselah passed in this world? their whole duration seems, at this distance, in the words of St. James, 'Even as a vapor that appeareth for a little time, and then vanisheth away.'

"It will therefore be the same with me. I know not how long I shall live here below, perhaps I shall see but a portion of this year, and shall enter into glory before it is concluded; or perhaps I shall yet see many more years. This the Lord knows, and I ought not to consider that such knowledge would be of any importance to me, since that which constitutes my *life*, is not its length or duration, but the use which is made of it.

"It is to Jesus, then, that all my life must be devoted, without him I can do nothing. 'My life is hid with Christ in God.' He has 'bought me with a price,' I ought, therefore, 'to glorify God in my body, and in my spirit, which are God's.'

"Truly to live is to know, that my thoughts and actions are all directed to the glory of Jesus, whether upon earth by faith and hope, or in heaven by the sight and by the glory of God.

"But here below, I have only time at my disposal; that is to say, days composed of hours or rather, I have in reality but a single day to make use of. Yesterday is no longer mine, and to-morrow, where is it? I have it not yet, and perhaps shall never see it.

"Lo my earthly life is 'to-day.' What must I do then with 'to-day,' that God may be honored and glorified in it? for after all, if I have the happiness of counting the year 1844, as dating from a Christian era, and not from that of a false prophet with the Mahomedans, nor yet of a false God, with the poor Indians, it must be to Jesus Christ, from whose birth I count my years, that those years should be dedicated.

"Here I am, therefore, in the presence of my Saviour, of whom I implore the Spirit of wisdom and prudence to guide me in the employment of this my day, since in reality I have but one, and that is, 'To-day.'

"But I cannot do better than walk in the footsteps of my Redeemer, and in his conduct and conversation whilst on earth, I observe these three things: Temperance, piety, and charity, to all of which he wholly devoted himself, and has thus left me an example to follow.

"I will therefore imitate him first in his temperance. He rose early in the morning--he eat frugally--he worked diligently--he wearied himself in well-doing: in a word, he exerted the whole strength of his mind and body in the cause of truth, but never in the cause of evil.

"These, therefore, must be settled rules, moderate sleep, moderate repasts, moderate care and attention to the body; active employment, always to a useful purpose, profitable to my neighbor, and never interfering with my duties at home.

"In the next place, I must imitate Jesus in His **piety**. His Father's will was as His daily food. What a thought! To live wholly to God, and as He himself teaches us in His Holy Word. To do this, I must know His Word; I must study it, meditate upon it, and learn it by heart. Besides reading, I must pray, for prayer is the life both of my heart and soul with God. What glory is thus permitted to me, a poor sinner, that I **ought**, and that I **can**, live to Him, love Him, and devote myself to Him! It is heaven already begun on earth; for in heaven my soul will enjoy no other happiness than that of knowing God, and living to His glory. This thought fills me with joy, and I am encouraged by it to consecrate myself wholly to Him, as did my Lord and Saviour.

"Lastly, I will, by the grace of God, imitate Jesus in his **charity**. How many souls there are about me to love, to comfort, to enlighten and to assist. But I can only do it in the measure which God himself has assigned to me. At my age, and but a girl, subject to the wishes of my parents, I ought only to desire to do good in proportion to the means with which the Lord has furnished me. But I must, in so doing, endeavor to overcome selfishness, idleness, the love of ease, avarice, hardness of heart, pride, and indifference, and I must love my neighbor as myself. Oh! what an important undertaking, and how many excuses and deceits this kind of charity will encounter and overcome.

"But I will look to Jesus, and pray to him; I will implore the secret guidance of his Spirit; and since he is faithful, he will not leave me alone, but will lead me, and enable me to walk day by day, I mean 'to-day,' in his sight, and in communion with him, who is so full of love and gentleness."

This, my dear Esther, is what I have copied from Amelia's journal. You see the light in which our friend regarded her life on earth, and how much importance she attached to one *day*--a single day.

As I read what she had written, I felt my soul humbled before God, and I trembled to think of the useless way in which I had hitherto spent my time.

You see in particular what Amelia felt on the subject of piety; what love her soul had for God! and this is what produced in her that active, sincere, and constant charity.

You cannot form the least idea of the work, of kindness and benevolence which she was enabled to accomplish. That passage, "The memory of the just is blessed," is truly applicable to her.

Amelia was justified in her Saviour, for she trusted in him, and thus was she also justified before God, by her faith in Jesus. The spirit of Jesus led her in "all her way," and in whatever family she appeared, her actions and words manifested a heavenly mind.

Her name is remembered with blessing in the hearts of all who knew her; her counsels, her instructions, her example, and her acts of benevolence, are continually spoken of by those who witnessed them, and it is thus that she left behind a sweet savor of holiness, like a ray of heavenly light.

Dear Esther, here is an example placed before us; it has been the will of God that we should know her, that we might be charmed with her excellence, and that the happiness both of her life and death, might tempt us to imitate her.

No, no, my sister, she is not dead; she is rather, as the poor workman said, at her grave, "a child of God in heaven." As *she* followed Jesus, let us also follow her, and let her memory be thus a blessing to us both.

God be with you, my dear sister. I long to see you, that we may pray the Lord together, to make us like his faithful, holy servant, the dear and pious Amelia.

Yours, &c.,
ANNA.

IV.
The Tract found by the Way-Side.

"Take away the dross from the silver, and there shall come forth a vessel for the finer." --Prov. XXV. 4.

Every one knows in these days what is meant by a ***religious tract***. It is a little printed pamphlet, which is sold at a very low price, or is still oftener given away, or dropped in the streets and lanes, that those who either purchase, or accept, or find them, may read the truths of the Gospel, and the good advice which they contain.

This is an old-fashioned way of imparting instruction, both to high and low. It was in use, for instance, as early as the first days of the Reformation, when some faithful Christians of Picardy, in France, assembled together to read the Holy Scriptures, on which account they were exposed to persecution, death, and above all, to be burnt alive.

These true disciples of the Lord Jesus composed and distributed, with considerable difficulty, some little pamphlets, in which were taught the doctrines of salvation by Christ alone, and in a form which enabled the poor and ignorant to read and understand; for it was impossible for them at that time to procure a Bible, which was not only a scarce book, but cost a large sum of money: indeed, almost as much as a thousand Bibles would cost in the present day, and which, besides, they could not carry home and read quietly to themselves, as they were able to do with a simple tract.

At a later period, and chiefly for the last fifty years, this method has been adopted in almost all countries where true Christian churches and societies have been established; and even now, millions of these tracts, adapted to all ages and conditions of men, are published and distributed every year.

It is, however, but too true, that many tracts thus distributed are not *religious tracts*; that is to say, the substance of them is not in conformity with the truth of scripture. Many are published for the purpose of upholding false religion and wicked principles, and which, consequently, do great mischief to those who read them.

And if it be asked, "How can a good tract be distinguished from a bad one?" we thus reply to this very natural question.

A *good tract* is that which leads us to the Bible; which speaks of the love of God in Christ; and which encourages the reader to be holy from a motive of love to God.

A *bad tract* is therefore that which does not speak of the Bible; which tells us that salvation may be obtained by human merit, and which consequently would persuade us to be religious from interested motives: that is to say, to obtain pardon by means of our own good works.

Those tracts, too, which speak of man's happiness as if it came from man alone, and not from God, and which consequently deny the truth of God's word: these must also be called *bad tracts*, and must therefore be carefully avoided.

The good that is done by the distribution of good tracts, can scarcely be believed. There are many families, even in prosperity, who never tasted real happiness until some of these evangelical writings found their way amongst them. The following anecdote is an interesting proof of this:

The family of a vinedresser, in the Canton of Vaud, in Switzerland, was, unhappily, as well known in the village in which he lived, for his bad conduct, as for his impiety. The father, whose name we will not mention, was a proud and hard-hearted man, both intemperate and dissolute; and his wife, who thought as little of the fear of God as her husband did, was what might be called a *noisy babbler*.

The pastor of the village had often, but vainly, endeavored to lead these unhappy people to a sense of religion, but he was always received by them with scoffing and ridicule.

The family was composed of the vinedresser's three children. The eldest, Mark, was as haughty as his father, and although he was only fourteen years of age, he was already able to join in the disorders of his drunken and gaming companions. He was entirely devoid of any sense of religion. His sister, Josephine, who was rather more than twelve years old, possessed a more amiable disposition. The pastor's wife took much interest in this child, who could not help seeing that her parents were not guided by the Spirit of God. Peter, the youngest, was but ten years of age, but his brother's wicked example counteracted all the good which he might have received from that of his more amiable sister.

About the end of May, there was to be, in a village not far distant, a match at rifle-shooting. It was a public fete, at which all the people in the neighborhood assembled.

On the morning of this day, Mark had answered his father with great insolence, at which he was so much enraged, that he punished him severely, and forbad him, besides, to go to the fete. The father went thither himself, and Mark, after a moment's indecision, determined not to heed the command he had received, but to follow him to the shooting-match.

He therefore took advantage of his mother's absence, who, according to her usual custom, was gone to gossip with some of her neighbors, and notwithstanding the remonstrances of Josephine, he hastened over fields and hedges, to the scene of the match.

"What is this?" cried he, picking up a little pamphlet, with a cover of colored paper, which was lying on the path near the opening in the hedge. "Oh! it is one of those tracts they leave about everywhere; it will do very well to load my gun;" and so saying, he put the tract into his pocket, and ran on as before.

But when he approached the village where they were shooting, dancing, playing, and making a great noise, he suddenly stopped, for he recollected that if he should meet with his father, who was there, he would certainly beat him, and send him home again, in presence of all the people who might be assembled; besides, his brother Peter was there also, and he might see him, and tell his father. He therefore kept at a distance, behind a hedge, not daring to advance any farther.

"Supposing I read this book!" said he, at last, after having vainly racked his brain to find out how he could be at the fete without being discovered. "There is nothing in it but nonsense, I know beforehand; however, it will occupy me for a while."

This tract was called "The Happy Family," and Mark became so much interested in it, that he not only read the whole, but many parts of it twice over.

"How odd it is," said he, when he had finished reading; "I should never have thought it could be thus; this Andrew and Julia, after all, were much happier than we are, and than I am, in particular. Ah!" added he, as he walked on by the hedge-side, looking on the ground, "possibly Josephine may have spoken the truth, and that, after all, the right way is the one which this lady points out."

As he thought over the little story he had been reading, he retraced his steps towards his own village, at first rather slowly, but soon at a quicker pace, and he entered his father's house very quietly, and without either whistling or making a noise, as he generally did.

"You have not then been to the fete," said Josephine.

Mark.--(A little ashamed.)--"I dared not go, I was afraid my father would beat me."

Josephine.--"It would have been better, Mark, if you had been equally afraid of offending God."

Mark was on the point of ridiculing her, as he always did, but he recollected Andrew and Julia, and was silent.

Josephine.--(Kindly.)--"But is it not true, Mark? would it not be better to fear God, than to be always offending him?"

Mark.--(Knitting his brow.)--"Yes, as Andrew and Julia did! would it not?"

Josephine.--(surprised.)--"Of whom do you speak, Mark? Is it of "The Happy Family," in which an Andrew and a Julia are mentioned. Have you ever read that beautiful story?"

"Here it is," said Mark, drawing the tract from his pocket, and giving it to his sister.

Josephine.--"Yes, this is it, exactly! But brother, where did you get it, for it is quite new; did you buy it of a *Scripture Reader*."

"Did I *buy* it?" said Mark, sullenly. "Do you suppose I should spend my money in such nonsense as *that?*"

Josephine.--"Then how did you get it? Did any one give it you?"

Mark.--(Slyly.)--"Ah! they have often tried to give me some, but I tore them to pieces, and threw them away, before their faces!"

Josephine.--"So much the worse, Mark! for the truth of God is written in them, and it is very sinful to tear the truth of God in pieces."

Mark.--(Rudely.)--"But you see I have not torn this, for it is quite whole! And as you are so anxious to know how I came by it, I found it on the ground, near the road, and just beyond the brushwood."

Josephine.--"Ah! then I know where it came from. The Pastor's son, and the two sons of the schoolmaster, have got up a Religious Tract Society, who distribute them in all directions."

Mark.--(Reproachfully.)--"And pray why do they scatter them about in this way? Can't they leave people alone, without cramming every body's head with their own fancies. Let them keep their religion to themselves, and leave other people to do the same."

Josephine.--"Do you think, Mark, that Andrew and Julia did wrong to listen to their father and grandmamma, and to follow the precepts of the Bible in preference to the ridicule of scoffers."

Mark.--(Softened.)--"I did not say *that*.... I think Andrew and Julia were right; but ... come give me back the Tract; I want to look at something in it again."

Mark then went away, carrying the Tract with him; and shortly after, Josephine saw him sitting in the garden, behind a hedge of sweet- briar, reading it attentively.

"Where's that good-for-nothing Mark?" demanded the vinedresser, when he returned home at night half tipsy. "Did he dare to venture to the shooting-match? I was told that he was seen sneaking about the outskirts of the village! where is he now?"

"He went to bed more than an hour ago," answered his mother, "and was no more at the shooting-match than I was, for I saw him reading in the garden."

"Mark, *reading*!" replied his father. "What could he be reading? It would be a miracle to see him with a book in his hand. An idle fellow like him, who never did learn any thing, and never will!"

The vinedresser's wife was silent, and after putting poor little Peter to bed, who was quite tired and weary, she managed to get the father to bed also, and peace reigned for a season in this miserable abode.

Mark, however, who was not asleep when his father returned, had heard himself called a good-for-nothing idle fellow, and he trembled from head to foot, when he found he had been seen in the neighborhood of the village.

"What a good thing it was," said he to himself, "that I did not go on! It was certainly God who prevented me!" added he, half ashamed of the thought because it was so new to him; but he determined no longer to resist it.

On the morrow, to the great surprise of his father and mother, Mark got up in good humor; he answered his father without grumbling, and when he was desired to go and work in the field, Mark hastened to take his hoe and spade, and set off, singing merrily.

"What has happened to him?" asked the father. "One would scarcely believe it was he! Wife, what did you say to him yesterday, to make him so good-humored this morning?"

"I never even spoke to him," said his wife, dryly. "You know how whimsical he is."

"I wish he may remain in his present mind!" said the vinedresser; and thereupon he went off to the ale-house, to talk with his neighbors of the best shots of the preceding day.

Josephine related the history of the little tract to the good pastor's wife, who advised her to meet Mark on his return from the field, and to speak to him again of what he had read.

"Is it *you*, sister?" said Mark, in a happy tone of voice, as soon as he saw her. "It is very good of you to meet me."

Josephine, who never received such a welcome from him before, was quite delighted, and going up to him, she said, affectionately, "I want very much to talk with you again about Andrew and Julia."

Mark.--(Seriously.)--"And so do I. I should like very much to resemble them."

Josephine.--(Quickly.)--"Do you mean what you say, Mark? Have you thought of it again since yesterday?"

Mark.--(Still serious.)--"I have thought so much about it, that I am determined to change my habits. Yes, Josephine, I think you are right, and that, after all, religion is better than ridicule."

The conversation continued as it had commenced, and when Mark returned home, he went up and kissed his mother, who was just laying the table for dinner.

"What's the matter?" said she, with some surprise; "you seem in very good spirits, today."

"Nothing is the matter, good mother, but that I wish to alter my conduct," replied Mark, seriously.

"To alter your conduct," cried little Peter, as he looked up in his brother's face, and began to titter.

"And you, too, little Peter," said Mark, "you must become good, also."

"What a funny idea," cried the child, laughing. "**What** has made you turn schoolmaster, all at once? and, pray, when am I to begin?"

"We shall see by-and-bye," said Mark, kindly. "In the meantime, come and help me to tend the cow."

"There is something behind all this!" said the mother and she blushed to think that this change had not been occasioned by anything she had said or done to him, herself.

When the father returned from the ale-house, they all sat down to dinner, and as usual, without saying "*grace*." Josephine said hers to herself, and Mark, who recollected Andrew and Julia, blushed when he took his spoon to eat his soup.

After dinner, when they were out of the house, Josephine said to Mark, "What a pity it is, brother, that papa does not pray before each meal."

"All *that* will come in time, Josephine," said Mark; "I never prayed myself, and yet ... I must now begin directly. But what shall I do? Papa will be very angry if he sees me religious."

"I do not think he will," said Josephine, "for I heard him say to mumma, this morning, that he should be very glad if your conduct improved."

Mark blushed, but did not reply. He returned to his work without being desired to do so, and his father, who was quite astonished, said to his wife, "There is something very extraordinary about Mark. I wish it may last."

"You wish it may last!" said his wife; "how can you wish that, when you do not care to improve yourself."

"And you, my poor wife," said the vinedresser, "do you care to change any more than I do? I think as to that matter, we cannot say much against each other."

"Well, at all events," said his wife, "I am not a drunkard."

"Nor am I a tattler," replied the husband. "And for this reason let us each think of our own fault, and if Mark is disposed to reform, do not let us prevent him; for, my poor wife, *our* example is not a very good one for him."

Josephine, who was working at her needle, in the adjoining room, could not help overhearing this confession of her father, and she felt the more encouraged to uphold Mark in his good intention.

She therefore went again to meet him, and repeated to him all she had heard. "I think," added she, "you will do well to relate what has happened to our father and mother, and read them the little tract."

"Not yet," said Mark, "for my principles are not sufficiently strong. It is but an hour since the ale-house keeper's son laughed at me, because I told him I would not play at nine-pins with him, during working hours. He asked me if I was becoming a Methodist, and I did not know what answer to make. However, I trust I am already improving, and I have read the little tract again for the third time."

"Oh!" said Josephine, "we ought to read the Bible, and we do not possess one."

"True," said Mark, somewhat surprised. "I never thought of *that*. We have really no Bible in the house! Indeed, this must not be," he added, looking on the ground, and striking it with his spade.

"What shall we do, then?" said Josephine, "for it would be very nice to have one."

Mark became thoughtful, but said nothing. From that day his conduct was always regular, and his habits industrious, so much so, that his father, who was never in the habit of showing him much kindness, said to him, at the dinner table, and before all the rest of the family, "Well, my good Mark, tell us what has happened to you; for it is very pleasant to us to see how well you now behave. Tell us, my boy, what has been the cause of this improvement."

"It was from this book," said Mark, drawing it out of his pocket, where he always kept it.

"What book is it?" said his mother, scornfully. "Is it not some of that horrid trash, that"...

"Be silent," cried the father. "If this book has done good, how can it be horrid trash? Do sour grapes produce good wine?"

"But," replied the mother, bitterly, "I will not have any of those books and tracts in this house."

"Well, for my part," said the vinedresser, "I will encourage all that teach my children to do what is right. Mark has worked well for the last eight days; he has not occasioned me a moment's vexation during the whole of that time, and as he says that this book has been the means of his improvement, I shall also immediately read it myself. Come, Mark, let us hear it. You can read fluently; come, we will all listen. Wife, do you be quiet, and you too, Peter; as for Josephine she is quite ready."

Mark began to read, but he could not proceed far; his father got up and went out, without saying a word, and his mother began to remove the dinner-things.

But as soon as the family re-assembled in the evening, the father said to Mark, "Go on with your reading, Mark, I want to hear the end, for I like the story."

Mark read, and when he came to that part of the tract, in which the Bible is mentioned, the vinedresser looked up to a high shelf on the wall, where were some old books, and said, "wife, had we not once a Bible?"

"Fifteen years ago," she answered, "you exchanged it for a pistol."

The vinedresser blushed, and listened with out farther interruption until Mark had done reading. When the tract was finished, he remained silent, his head leaning on his hands, and his elbows on his knees. Josephine thought this was the time to speak about the Bible, which she had so long wished to possess, and she went up to her father, and stood for some time by his side without speaking.

Her father perceived her, and raising his head, he said to her, "What do you want, Josephine, tell me, my child, what do you want to ask me?"

"Dear papa," said the child, "I have long desired to read the Bible, would you be so kind as to buy me one?"

"A Bible," cried her mother, "what can *you* want with a Bible, at *your* age?"

"Oh! wife, wife," said the vinedresser, much vexed, "when will you help me to do what is right?" "Yes, my child," he added, kissing Josephine's cheek, "I will buy you one to-morrow. Do you think there are any to be had at the pastor's house?"

"Oh! yes, plenty," cried Josephine, "and very large ones too!"

"Very well then," said the father, as he got up, and went out of the house, "you shall have a very large one."

"But," said his wife, calling after him, "you don't know how much it will cost."

"It will not cost so much as the wine I mean no longer to drink!" replied the father, firmly.

He kept his word. The Bible was purchased on the morrow, and the same evening the father desired Mark to read him a whole chapter. The ale-house saw him no more the whole of that week, and still less the following Sunday. His friends laughed at him, and wanted to get him back. He was at first tempted and almost overcome, but the thought of the Bible restrained him, and he determined to refuse.

"Are you gone mad, then?" said they.

"No," replied he, "but I read the Bible now, and as it says, that drunkards shall not 'inherit the kingdom of God,' I listen to what it says, and I desire to cease to be a drunkard."

"You see," said Josephine to Mark, as they accompanied each other to church, "how good God has been to us. We have now a Bible, and it is read by all at home."

Mark.--"Have you been able to tell the pastor's son how much good his tract has done us?"

Josephine.--"I told his mother."

Mark.--"And what did she say?"

Josephine.--"She said, 'God is wonderful in all his ways,' and that, 'He which hath begun the good work in us, will perform it until the day of Jesus Christ.'"

Mark.--(Feelingly.)--"Who could have thought that when I went as a rebel to that Fete, that God was there waiting to draw me to himself. But, dear Josephine, there is yet much to be done."

"But," said Josephine, "where God has promised he is also able to perform. He has told us to pray in the name of the Lord Jesus Christ. Let us do so, and you will see that God will renew our hearts, and make us wise and good."

The Codes Of Hammurabi And Moses
W. W. Davies

QTY

The discovery of the Hammurabi Code is one of the greatest achievements of archaeology, and is of paramount interest, not only to the student of the Bible, but also to all those interested in ancient history...

Religion   **ISBN:** *1-59462-338-4*   **Pages:132**
MSRP $12.95

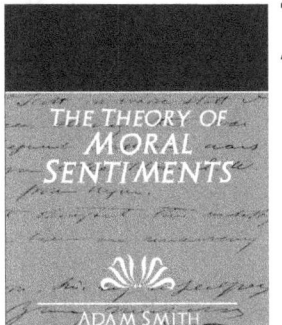

The Theory of Moral Sentiments
Adam Smith

QTY

This work from 1749. contains original theories of conscience amd moral judgment and it is the foundation for systemof morals.

Philosophy **ISBN:** *1-59462-777-0*   **Pages:536**
MSRP $19.95

Jessica's First Prayer
Hesba Stretton

QTY

In a screened and secluded corner of one of the many railway-bridges which span the streets of London there could be seen a few years ago, from five o'clock every morning until half past eight, a tidily set-out coffee-stall, consisting of a trestle and board, upon which stood two large tin cans, with a small fire of charcoal burning under each so as to keep the coffee boiling during the early hours of the morning when the work-people were thronging into the city on their way to their daily toil...

Pages:84

Childrens   **ISBN:** *1-59462-373-2*   *MSRP $9.95*

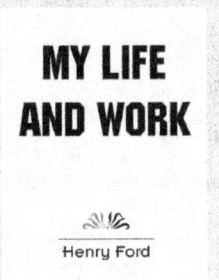

My Life and Work
Henry Ford

QTY

Henry Ford revolutionized the world with his implementation of mass production for the Model T automobile. Gain valuable business insight into his life and work with his own auto-biography... "We have only started on our development of our country we have not as yet, with all our talk of wonderful progress, done more than scratch the surface. The progress has been wonderful enough but..."

Pages:300

Biographies/   **ISBN:** *1-59462-198-5*   *MSRP $21.95*

The Art of Cross-Examination
Francis Wellman

QTY

I presume it is the experience of every author, after his first book is published upon an important subject, to be almost overwhelmed with a wealth of ideas and illustrations which could readily have been included in his book, and which to his own mind, at least, seem to make a second edition inevitable. Such certainly was the case with me; and when the first edition had reached its sixth impression in five months, I rejoiced to learn that it seemed to my publishers that the book had met with a sufficiently favorable reception to justify a second and considerably enlarged edition. ...

Reference   **ISBN:** *1-59462-647-2*

Pages:412

MSRP $19.95

On the Duty of Civil Disobedience
Henry David Thoreau

QTY

Thoreau wrote his famous essay, On the Duty of Civil Disobedience, as a protest against an unjust but popular war and the immoral but popular institution of slave-owning. He did more than write—he declined to pay his taxes, and was hauled off to gaol in consequence. Who can say how much this refusal of his hastened the end of the war and of slavery ?

Law   **ISBN:** *1-59462-747-9*

Pages:48

MSRP $7.45

Dream Psychology
Psychoanalysis for Beginners

Sigmund Freud

Dream Psychology Psychoanalysis for Beginners
Sigmund Freud

QTY

Sigmund Freud, born Sigismund Schlomo Freud (May 6, 1856 - September 23, 1939), was a Jewish-Austrian neurologist and psychiatrist who co-founded the psychoanalytic school of psychology. Freud is best known for his theories of the unconscious mind, especially involving the mechanism of repression; his redefinition of sexual desire as mobile and directed towards a wide variety of objects; and his therapeutic techniques, especially his understanding of transference in the therapeutic relationship and the presumed value of dreams as sources of insight into unconscious desires.

Psychology   **ISBN:** *1-59462-905-6*

Pages:196

MSRP $15.45

The Miracle of Right Thought
Orison Swett Marden

QTY

Believe with all of your heart that you will do what you were made to do. When the mind has once formed the habit of holding cheerful, happy, prosperous pictures, it will not be easy to form the opposite habit. It does not matter how improbable or how far away this realization may see, or how dark the prospects may be, if we visualize them as best we can, as vividly as possible, hold tenaciously to them and vigorously struggle to attain them, they will gradually become actualized, realized in the life. But a desire, a longing without endeavor, a yearning abandoned or held indifferently will vanish without realization.

Self Help   **ISBN:** *1-59462-644-8*

Pages:360

MSRP $25.45

QTY

The Rosicrucian Cosmo-Conception Mystic Christianity *by Max Heindel*   ISBN: *1-59462-188-8*   **$38.95**
The Rosicrucian Cosmo-conception is not dogmatic, neither does it appeal to any other authority than the reason of the student. It is; not controversial, but is: sent forth in the, hope that it may help to clear... New Age/Religion Pages 646

Abandonment To Divine Providence *by Jean-Pierre de Caussade*   ISBN: *1-59462-228-0*   **$25.95**
"The Rev. Jean Pierre de Caussade was one of the most remarkable spiritual writers of the Society of Jesus in France in the 18th Century. His death took place at Toulouse in 1751. His works have gone through many editions and have been republished... Inspirational/Religion Pages 400

Mental Chemistry *by Charles Haanel*   ISBN: *1-59462-192-6*   **$23.95**
Mental Chemistry allows the change of material conditions by combining and appropriately utilizing the power of the mind. Much like applied chemistry creates something new and unique out of careful combinations of chemicals the mastery of mental chemistry... New Age Pages 354

The Letters of Robert Browning and Elizabeth Barret Barrett 1845-1846 vol II   ISBN: *1-59462-193-4*   **$35.95**
by Robert Browning and Elizabeth Barrett Biographies Pages 596

Gleanings In Genesis (volume I) *by Arthur W. Pink*   ISBN: *1-59462-130-6*   **$27.45**
Appropriately has Genesis been termed "the seed plot of the Bible" for in it we have, in germ form, almost all of the great doctrines which are afterwards fully developed in the books of Scripture which follow... Religion/Inspirational Pages 420

The Master Key *by L. W. de Laurence*   ISBN: *1-59462-001-6*   **$30.95**
In no branch of human knowledge has there been a more lively increase of the spirit of research during the past few years than in the study of Psychology, Concentration and Mental Discipline. The requests for authentic lessons in Thought Control, Mental Discipline and... New Age/Business Pages 422

The Lesser Key Of Solomon Goetia *by L. W. de Laurence*   ISBN: *1-59462-092-X*   **$9.95**
This translation of the first book of the "Lernegton" which is now for the first time made accessible to students of Talismanic Magic was done, after careful collation and edition, from numerous Ancient Manuscripts in Hebrew, Latin, and French... New Age/Occult Pages 92

Rubaiyat Of Omar Khayyam *by Edward Fitzgerald*   ISBN:*1-59462-332-5*   **$13.95**
Edward Fitzgerald, whom the world has already learned, in spite of his own efforts to remain within the shadow of anonymity, to look upon as one of the rarest poets of the century, was born at Bredfield, in Suffolk, on the 31st of March, 1809. He was the third son of John Purcell... Music Pages 172

Ancient Law *by Henry Maine*   ISBN: *1-59462-128-4*   **$29.95**
The chief object of the following pages is to indicate some of the earliest ideas of mankind, as they are reflected in Ancient Law, and to point out the relation of those ideas to modern thought. Religion/History Pages 452

Far-Away Stories *by William J. Locke*   ISBN: *1-59462-129-2*   **$19.45**
"Good wine needs no bush, but a collection of mixed vintages does. And this book is just such a collection. Some of the stories I do not want to remain buried for ever in the museum files of dead magazine-numbers an author's not unpardonable vanity..." Fiction Pages 272

Life of David Crockett *by David Crockett*   ISBN: *1-59462-250-7*   **$27.45**
"Colonel David Crockett was one of the most remarkable men of the times in which he lived. Born in humble life, but gifted with a strong will, an indomitable courage, and unremitting perseverance... Biographies/New Age Pages 424

Lip-Reading *by Edward Nitchie*   ISBN: *1-59462-206-X*   **$25.95**
Edward B. Nitchie, founder of the New York School for the Hard of Hearing, now the Nitchie School of Lip-Reading, Inc, wrote "LIP-READING Principles and Practice". The development and perfecting of this meritorious work on lip-reading was an undertaking... How-to Pages 400

A Handbook of Suggestive Therapeutics, Applied Hypnotism, Psychic Science   ISBN: *1-59462-214-0*   **$24.95**
by Henry Munro Health/New Age/Health/Self-help Pages 376

A Doll's House: and Two Other Plays *by Henrik Ibsen*   ISBN: *1-59462-112-8*   **$19.95**
Henrik Ibsen created this classic when in revolutionary 1848 Rome. Introducing some striking concepts in playwriting for the realist genre, this play has been studied the world over. Fiction/Classics/Plays 308

The Light of Asia *by sir Edwin Arnold*   ISBN: *1-59462-204-3*   **$13.95**
In this poetic masterpiece, Edwin Arnold describes the life and teachings of Buddha. The man who was to become known as Buddha to the world was born as Prince Gautama of India but he rejected the worldly riches and abandoned the reigns of power when... Religion/History/Biographies Pages 170

The Complete Works of Guy de Maupassant *by Guy de Maupassant*   ISBN: *1-59462-157-8*   **$16.95**
"For days and days, nights and nights, I had dreamed of that first kiss which was to consecrate our engagement, and I knew not on what spot I should put my lips..." Fiction/Classics Pages 240

The Art of Cross-Examination *by Francis L. Wellman*   ISBN: *1-59462-309-0*   **$26.95**
Written by a renowned trial lawyer, Wellman imparts his experience and uses case studies to explain how to use psychology to extract desired information through questioning. How-to/Science/Reference Pages 408

Answered or Unanswered? *by Louisa Vaughan*   ISBN: *1-59462-248-5*   **$10.95**
Miracles of Faith in China Religion Pages 112

The Edinburgh Lectures on Mental Science (1909) *by Thomas*   ISBN: *1-59462-008-3*   **$11.95**
This book contains the substance of a course of lectures recently given by the writer in the Queen Street Hall, Edinburgh. Its purpose is to indicate the Natural Principles governing the relation between Mental Action and Material Conditions... New Age/Psychology Pages 148

Ayesha *by H. Rider Haggard*   ISBN: *1-59462-301-5*   **$24.95**
Verily and indeed it is the unexpected that happens! Probably if there was one person upon the earth from whom the Editor of this, and of a certain previous history, did not expect to hear again... Classics Pages 380

Ayala's Angel *by Anthony Trollope*   ISBN: *1-59462-352-X*   **$29.95**
The two girls were both pretty, but Lucy who was twenty-one who supposed to be simple and comparatively unattractive, whereas Ayala was credited, as her Bombwhat romantic name might show, with poetic charm and a taste for romance. Ayala when her father died was nineteen... Fiction Pages 484

The American Commonwealth *by James Bryce*   ISBN: *1-59462-286-8*   **$34.45**
An interpretation of American democratic political theory. It examines political mechanics and society from the perspective of Scotsman James Bryce Politics Pages 572

Stories of the Pilgrims *by Margaret P. Pumphrey*   ISBN: *1-59462-116-0*   **$17.95**
This book explores pilgrims religious oppression in England as well as their escape to Holland and eventual crossing to America on the Mayflower, and their early days in New England... History Pages 268

www.bookjungle.com *email: sales@bookjungle.com fax: 630-214-0564 mail: Book Jungle PO Box 2226 Champaign, IL 61825*

QTY

The Fasting Cure *by Sinclair Upton*
ISBN: *1-59462-222-1* **$13.95**

In the Cosmopolitan Magazine for May, 1910, and in the Contemporary Review (London) for April, 1910, I published an article dealing with my experiences in fasting. I have written a great many magazine articles, but never one which attracted so much attention... New Age/Self Help/Health Pages 164

Hebrew Astrology *by Sepharial*
ISBN: *1-59462-308-2* **$13.45**

In these days of advanced thinking it is a matter of common observation that we have left many of the old landmarks behind and that we are now pressing forward to greater heights and to a wider horizon than that which represented the mind-content of our progenitors... Astrology Pages 144

Thought Vibration or The Law of Attraction in the Thought World
ISBN: *1-59462-127-6* **$12.95**

by William Walker Atkinson
Psychology/Religion Pages 144

Optimism *by Helen Keller*
ISBN: *1-59462-108-X* **$15.95**

Helen Keller was blind, deaf, and mute since 19 months old, yet famously learned how to overcome these handicaps, communicate with the world, and spread her lectures promoting optimism. An inspiring read for everyone... Biographies/Inspirational Pages 84

Sara Crewe *by Frances Burnett*
ISBN: *1-59462-360-0* **$9.45**

In the first place, Miss Minchin lived in London. Her home was a large, dull, tall one, in a large, dull square, where all the houses were alike, and all the sparrows were alike, and where all the door-knockers made the same heavy sound... Childrens/Classic Pages 88

The Autobiography of Benjamin Franklin *by Benjamin Franklin*
ISBN: *1-59462-135-7* **$24.95**

The Autobiography of Benjamin Franklin has probably been more extensively read than any other American historical work, and no other book of its kind has had such ups and downs of fortune. Franklin lived for many years in England, where he was agent... Biographies/History Pages 332

Name	
Email	
Telephone	
Address	
City, State ZIP	

☐ **Credit Card**   ☐ **Check / Money Order**

Credit Card Number	
Expiration Date	
Signature	

Please Mail to: Book Jungle
PO Box 2226
Champaign, IL 61825
or Fax to: 630-214-0564

ORDERING INFORMATION

web: *www.bookjungle.com*
email: *sales@bookjungle.com*
fax: *630-214-0564*
mail: *Book Jungle PO Box 2226 Champaign, IL 61825*
or PayPal *to sales@bookjungle.com*

Please contact us for bulk discounts

DIRECT-ORDER TERMS

**20% Discount if You Order
Two or More Books**
Free Domestic Shipping!
Accepted: Master Card, Visa,
Discover, American Express

www.ingramcontent.com/pod-product-compliance
Lightning Source LLC
Chambersburg PA
CBHW081159170626
46813CB00009B/3246